Gwion Dubh,

Druid Investigator

'With Druids, detection and dodgy dames, this is a real treat!'

-Liz Williams,
Author of BANNER OF SOULS, shortlisted for the
Arthur C Clarke Award 2006)

Gwion Dubh;

Druid Investigator

Containing
The case of the meddling honey
A case of the blast from the past

by
Penny Billington
Illustrated by Arthur Billington

Published by Appleseed Press

First published in Great Britain in 2007
by Appleseed Press, Essex SS1 7TA

This edition Createspace 20015
https://www.createspace.com

Text copyright © Penny Billington 2007
Illustrations copyright © Arthur Billington 2007

The right of Penny Billington and Arthur Billington to be
identified as the author and illustrator of this work has been
asserted.

www.pennybillington.co.uk

A catalogue record for this book is available from the British
Library

ISBN 978-0-9548572-2-6

To our parents,
And to the forest that never sleeps
PB & GD

CONTENTS

One: *The case of the Meddling honey*

Two: *The Case of the blast from the past*

1
Into the wide green yonder...

It was a mild night in the forest that never sleeps.
Below the dark sky, the heart of the deep wood holds
its secrets. But one lone Druid has made it his job to
plumb them. I moved... cautiously.
Gwion Dubh: Druid investigator.
Yep, that's Dubh, pronounced 'Duv'.
Those Celts have a lot to answer for.

So, what the hell (no, Druids don't believe in that place,
as you're asking) sort of work does a Druid Gumshoe
do? Well, pretty well anything. But the booze, broads
and in flagrante delicto bread and butter stuff is for the
regular guys in the Yellow Pages. My missions come
from higher up, you might say. And crossing
dimensions might enter into it. Probably best not to ask
about the Big Boss at this stage. But on forest command,
he's at the top of the tree. When he pipes, you dance.

So here I was, out on my latest case: to investigate
strange anomalies in the food chain. And what the
flowering hellebore did that mean? Well, usually, the
big guys eat the small guys, but there's more small
guys, so everyone just keeps going along in a merry
dance – basically, at this stage, your guess is as good as
mine. Still, mine not to reason why...

I thumbed my belt, checking my wand for quick access.
Best to be sure. Last year's incident with a maverick
shaman had brought me perilously near to
transmigration, and these track-ways looked ripe for
booby traps.
I hitched up my Druid camouflage, tucking its skirts
into my belt: a reassuring clack of knife hitting hipflask

reminded me that I was carrying the two chief necessities of my job. An emergency smudge stick suspended on a thong round my neck and garden flare tucked into my boot completed my ensemble. Except for the shades of course. Did I ever trip over a tree root? Please: I am a professional. And the punters expect a certain image. With shades, a waft of smudge and a confidential manner I could milk a dryad for information so she'd disappear into her bark thinking we'd just had a pleasant flirt. Why the hipflask? Well, not all the denizens of the forest are so rarefied. Take gnomes, for example. Grumpy little mothers, most of them - it's all the wood chopping, and a chip on the shoulder, for which I don't blame them. By the time those Grimm brothers had finished their fairy stories hatchet job, the whole species was a laughing stock - hence the need for the aforementioned hipflask. Strictly not to be touched, you understand, except in case of dire emergency...

A silver moon shone through the trees, lighting my path. I tuned in and distinctly heard hedgepigs snuffling through leaf litter. Just underground and to my left, near the bole of a granddaddy oak I felt the vibrations of a badger about to break cover. All well so far. In the distance a she-fox shrieked and I felt my back hairs bristle. Reminded me of one Beltane night when I'd met up with a witchlet with a mission to improve interfaith relations, so we had an interlude investigating closer co-operation... It's a lonely job, and you're glad of all sentient contact, regardless of species. Excuse the digression; time can hang heavy and there's usually plenty of it for thinking. Until the corn sheaf hits the fan, as it eventually always does…

The night quietened as the hedgepigs went away. The oak dryad shivered and I was about to take the hint that

I'd been pressing the bark for long enough and should be on my way, when a new rustling came out of the stillness. I stepped up onto the tree's large bole and teetered a few inches above the forest floor as, within seconds, the undergrowth came alive with small mammals. Voles, shrews and mice swarmed over the leaf litter, taking no notice of my movements as I dragged the hem of my robe tightly around my ankles. No use looking for trouble.

After a few minutes watching them bustling, as at home in the open as a High Priest at a Sabbat, I realised that my mission was in front of my eyes. "Anomalies in the food chain'? Who'd've guessed that the boss could do corporate-speak? The Gwion translation, 'The vermin are getting antsy,' was about the size of it. The rodents were getting uppity.

Whoever had heard of fearless mice? And it looked like they'd been playing big-time whilst the cat was away. For a fearless mouse, every nook and cranny in the forest is honeymoon central with en-suite facilities; there were thousands.

Well, at least I knew the problem now. Predators; where were the predators? I stepped away from the oak, threatening the vole population with every step: I swear they looked annoyed as they dodged, and I knew I wouldn't get a wink of sleep that night or I'd wake bald and shaven with the feel of rodent teeth too near my throat for comfort.

With a shudder I jumped over a stoat in the nick of time. Stoats have had a bad press and, whilst not my totem animal, I do find them sympatico.

We share the same political affiliations, which are always a bond, and my blood boils over that eviction scandal... you must have seen it? At Toad Hall? All planned by that bloody Badger, of course. Don't tell me that the Rat or the Mole had the brains to repossess the old pile... Hmmm: too long in the woods alone, and you get to drifting off on these odd trains of thought.

So, let's get back to predators. At that very moment, the forest floor emptied. At lightning speed the rodents wheeled as one and disappeared under the leaf litter. Above me I heard the brazen clatter of a bird's wings and ducked instinctively as a giant owl flew over. The white flower-face with the stubby, wicked beak seemed to hold my gaze.

I'd seen owls looking wise, smug and disdainful before. Actually, the genus *bobo bobo* and I had history: hell, a beautiful tawny owl had given me the bum's rush, when I was a rookie. I'd needed a winged familiar before I set up in the sleuthing business and I still remember that owl's response to my request. You'd have thought I was a pellet she'd just regurgitated. So little Gwion was the only Druid on the block who setup his sleuthing business aided and abetted by a blackbird.

Tonight I got my revenge for that slight. I've seen horny, small, barn, eagle, long eared, screech and tawny owls, looking sniffy, snotty, smug and pretty sinister on occasion. But I have never seen an owl looking so confused. The undergrowth quivered: I don't often anthropomorphise, but I'll swear those hidden rodents were laughing.

The penny dropped. In sudden horror, I watched the flower-faced owl clatter back into the wood.
The owl; scourge of vermin. And why was that? *Because their flight is soundless,* that's why. Not with each feather rasping out a warning like a football rattle: that was

wrong, wrong, wrong. No wonder the mice were cocky - and reaching epidemic proportions. Noisy owls; it was a reversion of the natural order. Like polluting Druids or ego-less Magicians, if you get my drift. Who could have done such a horrible thing?

I hunkered down. How much further had this problem spread? I had some revealing powder in my wren-pochette. The elder branches above me rustled a warning as I produced a lighter: 'Yeh, yeh," I muttered over my shoulder to the dryad sitting on the lowest branch, as I sprinkled the powder in a circle. These trees with lineage - it' like going to dinner with a dowager duchess: they think you know nothing, so they're constantly checking you on stuff you learnt on the Druid foundation course. Ostentatiously I held the lighter at arm's length, so every dam' shrub with attitude could see what I was about, and that they were safe from the dread threat of fire. With a quick incantation some twigs became an Ogham sigil – part of our Druid tree alphabet magic - and I stood in the circle, waiting. The revealing powder began to glow... I was going to find out who had tampered with the natural order, and how.

OK, you're new to this, and I know the question everyone wants to ask. 'What's the spell?' But, unusually for an obliging guy, I'm not going to answer. You've got to appreciate that this stuff is my livelihood: you want in, you pay your dues and learn the hard way.
A few run-ins with astral canines and incarnations of Egyptian priests, you'll get to learn really fast, without cribbing my stock secrets. On some subjects, I stay mum.

So, what was out of kilter in this forest?

There had to have been a spell to knock out all the predator's hunting advantages: question was, how far had it gone? The circle glowed again, and as if in answer, the fox shrieked again. Mating. In August???? Another piece slotted into the jigsaw. Wrong, wrong, wrong. That fox wasn't calling, she was hunting, but something had forced an early warning device on her: her own cries. How sick was that? I wondered how many nights she'd barked out her warning. How thin was she now? I tuned into the ground, smudging a rabbit hole and laying full length on the ground. I could almost feel those plump little bodies, procreating like.... well, like rabbits: safe and warm in the dark; numbers growing, growing, growing as they hopped unconcernedly away from the warning bark of their main predator.

Below their burrow, curled abjectly when he should have been racing through the tunnels to stave off night starvation with a couple of bunny-burgers followed by slug surprise, I sensed a large badger. Seemed like he'd just given up.

Balance. Balance before all.
The natural order. It's a Druid thing.
The harmonies had been violated and, in its own way, and soon, the revealing magic would show me the perpetrators. I prepared for work.

2
Cottingley revisited...

I was sure that no animal could have masterminded this one: this sick mess had a different signature.

It didn't feel human either, so I ruled out a motley crew of latter-day hippies camped in an adjacent field. Earlier in the evening they'd come to set up their camp, a circus procession of tatterdemalion finery crashing through the undergrowth, alerting all the wildlife to flee well in advance. They'd come to a clearing - my clearing, incidentally, though I'd had plenty of warning to make myself scarce. They'd arranged themselves in a circle to meditate, lasted five minutes before the ants started biting and then rolled a joint, before an unearthly screech from high in the tree canopy set them running. I felt my wren pochette, in the pocket of which the remains of that joint nestled. I'd enjoy that, when this job was done. That screech had been one of my better impersonations, from a perfect vantage point in a squirrel's drey, high above the scene. Just a tip, don't copy me on that one. Anything worse than squirrel fleas, I don't want to experience it. And when squirrels throw nuts at you, you know you've been hit. I started to make a long cast round the periphery of the wood. I crept along the lonely tracks, one Druid gumshoe with a mission.

A quarter of the way round and I spotted, stark against the night sky, the gnarled boughs of an ancient hawthorn. She was huge and I could feel the aura from yards away - and she was noticing me, too. You've never been noticed by a tree? Don't you believe it!

Alarm bells rang.

I drew back into the shadow of the perimeter hedge and prepared to wait. It could be a long job, which was where half the contents of the hip flask came in. We all have our own definition of the term 'emergency'.

At about midnight I had my reward. A sudden faint sound of fiddles and a ray of light came from the deep shadows in the recesses of the bole of the hawthorn. It was the entrance to a fairy fort or rath, practically at my feet!

Quick as the paparazzi getting evidence of tantric occultism (Sunday Scandalsheet: 8th December 2010: I'm third from the left. It was a set up, but that's another story) I leapt behind a mature silver birch, shifting quickly after a twitching branch in a rude place alerted me to the toadstools getting squashed. I breathed in the tree, I breathed out the tree. I felt my adequate frame and robe coalescing with the aura of the bark: I knew I was becoming invisible, even to fairy eyes. Slowly I hunkered down in to a comfortable position and prepared to watch....

Out they popped, one by one, looking like extras from the Cottingley hoax. And, by the by, was that a triumph! Two little girls fooling the brains of the scientific world that cut-out fairies were real! And the joke is that, of course, the whole thing was actually real but impossible to prove. Don't ever try to get a fairy on film, my friend; you're on a hiding to nothing.

Anyway, the fairies who trooped out of this rath were all done up like Art Deco elfin tarts; bobbed hair and rouge, floaty draperies hiding the bare essentials...

I ask you. Why in Annwn (sorry if you're new to this, it's the Druidic Deep Otherworld – just ask if you need to – and pronounce it Ann-oon) would they do that?

Not for each other, that's for sure. Anything more workaday than a fairy in this season's pret-a-porter worktogs I have yet to see, and I've seen a few. We all know they like themed & fancy dress parties - with their life span, you've got to ring the changes - but only at special times; you know, Beltane – that's your Mayday - Midsummer, that sort of thing. These had obviously dressed up for a special reason. I resolved to follow them.

Gradually more and more poured out, so that the light surrounding them now resembled not so much the subdued glow of a Druid midwinter solstice rite, but the buzz and flash of a basement full of ritual magicians in full cry. This was incredible; the whole rath must be going out on a jolly.

I felt the soles of my shoes sink into the leaf litter and sparse grass; I could sense them resting on the invisible filaments of that largest living mass of plant material on the planet: the fungus. I eyed its fruits while the crowd jostled and noted my location: there'd be a good harvest of fly agaric to dry on another day and there's always a market for that stuff. Another day, another dollar.

Just when I thought they'd take all night getting ready, and started worrying about refreshing the disguise - tree aura's good, but the smell of we humans always comes to the fore eventually - one ugly little mother leapt onto a mouse and the shrill sound of a horn rang out. A mouse! Like a nightmare from the addled brain of Richard Dadd! They were really going for all the clichés tonight. A whole troop of mouse wranglers was now mounting as those in the vanguard set off. A full-blown fairy expedition with all the trappings could only mean one thing. They were going out to be seen.

On purpose.

And the only species stupid enough to believe that they really looked like that was, I hang my head in shame, my own. They were going to impress some humans.

I stayed hidden, communing with some boletus, friendliest of fungi, until they'd left the glade. There was no hurry; their trail would light up the atmosphere like fireflies on heat for a good half hour, and I couldn't risk being seen. When I found out what they were up to would be soon enough for the showdown.

I stood and stretched, pouring a little of the contents of my hipflask round the birch roots as a thank you: the hanging twigs caressed my face coquettishly and trunk bloomed extra silver: I made a mental note to return and look up one cool dryad when I'd finished the investigation.

Now, following a light approximately two feet above the ground whilst chanting concealment spells under your breath is not the quickest way to progress in the wood. Fortunately the shades saved me the worst of the glare, but that fairy trail shone like a beacon, plunging the path beneath into absolute darkness, so every young sapling with a sense of humour did its damnedest to trip me: before they clocked my knife, with which I nicked the bark of each that I stumbled over. I was busy now, but they got the message that, when I returned, it would be payback time. After that only a spiteful bramble got the better of me: brambles have no sense of cause and effect and this makes them dangerous adversaries.

I could almost hear the mice laughing as they dived for the shadows, out of the way of my crashing body.

There is nothing more infuriating than a derisory noise just beyond the scale of your hearing, and I followed the trail with renewed vigour.

This was getting more personal by the minute.

After about half a mile I ducked behind a gorse bush. The fairies who had been running with the mounted mice were now straggling and had come into view.

I lifted a small phial from my kestrel kit of spray-on self-repellent for all occasions, guaranteed to render one's personal olfactory signature neutralised to the habitat. I bent over to spray inside the cavernous folds of my robe and the gorse shoots nearest to me perked up noticeably, looking for a chance to prang me with their thorns: cheeky. A man could take offence. I coughed softly, not quite disguising my hissed "Shrubshag". This is the ultimate insult to a gorse, known for it's promiscuous flowering habit. It bridled.

With a smile, I followed the last of the fairy cavalcade to the extreme edge of the wood.

3
Dancing in the moonlight

Boy, oh, boy, oh boy! What a sight was there! A ring of tents and strange dwellings with asymmetric silhouettes against the sky: wigwams, yurts, tip-hurts, Yipis, marquadomes, all covered over with ragged tarpaulins: sort of Eastern European nomadic living meets the Wurzels, you know?

And in the centre - what a beacon fire! Blazing to the skies, with the entire colony of campers round it: very picturesque. I looked back at the wood. Even in the moonlight I could see patches where there should be dense black. This wood was beginning to look a little ragged round the edges, not to say ravaged. Bloody townies! Balance, remember me saying? It's a Druid thing.

But looking back at the innocent campfire scene I could almost forgive them; so must a tie-dyed Adam and Eve have played before the fall. They were sat in a circle - not even a space left where the prevailing breeze must surely have been periodically kippering at least three of them with the smoke. There was a lone guitar player strumming softly, and kettles were settled in the ashes, a respectable distance from the inferno. The host of the fairy folk were grouped half way up the field, making the stands of tall nettles and ragwort shimmer to my sensitised eyes, but it must have looked pitch black to the group blinded by the leaping flames.

The mood changed. Most of the campers were nursing cups of tea, but a few shifted and picked up drums as the guitarist struck a loud chord. I settled down for some serious g.b.h. of the ears, but actually, they were very good. And this was worrying.

This was obviously why the cavalcade was there. Don't ever think that that phrase *'a bridge between the worlds'* is a pretty metaphor. Bridges can be made, take my word, and music is a very effective tool: maybe the most magical. I heard a bridge of sound and rhythm being built that night, and saw the fairies begin to creep closer and closer to the musical invitation. Oh, oh.

OK, time for a bit of inter-species catch-up; just in case you're new to this sort of thing.

We live in a multidimensional world, right? Not only would you have to be deaf, dumb, blind & congenitally stupid not to acknowledge this, but if you don't, you undoubtedly wouldn't have read this far.

Now, let's leave aside the tree people, rock people, giant people and let's never, never even get on to the slug people. Let's concentrate on the fair or fairy folk and what people don't understand about them.

They are an alien species. They are not like humans. A simple fact, so easily overlooked, especially by... well, by that lot by the campfire, for example.

So, when you go out to build relationships, you ignore that fact at your peril. Like, if you're making pals with aliens, find out the rules that they're governed by. Martian, Venusian or fairy, those rules, I conjecture, will be different to ours. And so contact might not always be in our best interest. No judgment, no blame. Species are different, as anyone might find if not knowing the rules before engaging with the crocodile people. They may cry, but they ain't human.

Not that we're food for the fair folk; don't get me wrong. But us entering fairy can be very useful for them, and quite detrimental to our health.

Read your guidebooks, folks.

There are enough warnings in folk tales to put any sane seeker on the right lines, if you must persist.

By this time the drumming had plateaued out at quite a high pitch and several of the campers were dancing round the fire, swaying to the steady, hypnotic rhythm, carried along on the music like loaves to a Lughnasadh feast; an eerie thought, which I wished away hurriedly.

I took stock, leaning against the post of a barbed wire fence at the periphery of the wood. The fairy procession had advanced down the field and made a loose second circle around the dancers: I could feel them drinking in the music and breathing it out as strands of light which curled round the swaying form of the dancers; strands which I knew only too well could become restraints, given the right circumstances.

I fingered the joint again: maybe time for a quick toke whilst I saw how the situation developed? No, better keep a cool head - what?!! I jerked into full wakefulness. Where the hell had that thought come from? At a time when keeping my wits about me was crucial, why had I even thought of that? Now I'm a hardened operator, which just goes to show: faerie glamour is THAT seductive....

I leaned back on my hands and a friendly nettle gave me a good prickling: nothing like it for sharpening the focus. So what if they get a buzz from it, meaning it maliciously? Put it to good use, I thought, as I rubbed a smarting right palm.

Safely refocused, I took stock of the scene.

One little honey was swaying in front of the drummers now: eyes mostly closed, arms up to the sky, as if in - oh, Gods, as if in invocation. I stiffened and strained my ears.

"....Ohhhhhhhhh "(you know, the usual unearthly wailing stuff: de rigueur for the trainee shaman). This accounted for a good 16 bar intro: I was waiting for the guitar to go into a riff, but no such thing; the drums died down and I could hear quite clearly...

"Fair and free, from the hollow hills
Bless us as we surrender to your will..."

I didn't know whether to laugh or cry. Surrender to the bright hosts will! Give me strength!

As I watched, the faeries, obviously just waiting for the invitation, were infiltrating the energy fields of these babes in the wood. I could see their auras becoming semi-permeable, as faeries attached themselves.

The dancers and musicians were totally glamoured, and now I knew why the hunt lords had dragged themselves up: they were clearly visible on the edges of the group, dancing away merrily with wisps of drapery flying like something out of 'Fantasia' and distracting the campers' attention very nicely from the vampiric mauling they were getting from the near-invisible succubi.

This had to stop, but it was a tricky business. I was watching dangerous mischief and had a duty to intervene, but how - if at all - did this tie in with the balance of the food chain being disturbed? The rodent explosion was my prime objective, but this situation was now priority. Species solidarity ruled. I got ready for action.

4
Showtime!

I shifted. I'd removed my shades and the wren bag had provided me with a spyglass. I was totally on the case, so I know that the patch of ragwort I was by didn't warn me before I got another more vicious sting on the calf from the nettle. Weeds are a bloody nuisance, but they're loyal to their mates. Hissing "spring broth" at it - the nettle, you understand; don't go poisoning yourself with ragwort and pretend it's on my say-so - I cautiously advanced. Mind you, if I'd been lit up like Edward Woodward in the final-frame of the Wicker Man, the two groups would have been too involved to notice little Gwion.

That babe was wonderful! The main dancer; the crooner; the intoner; the invoker, for the Gods' sake. On the backburner of my awareness I clocked the long, brown, deer legs, fierce, hawk eyes, the mane of hair, salmon-like lissomness - she was a menagerie of totem animals all rolled into one.

But my immediate concern was her bear-like growling which led into more invocation.

"Let us be joined in brotherhood..." Oh brother! Have you ever been bullied by your brother? If you're doing this stuff, remember, choose your words carefully. I saw the vampire-faeries getting a further hold on the campers who, still mesmerized, had stopped dancing and were watching the glamour. It was a chariot race now, of four faeries with double mouse teams.

I'd missed a couple of verses, but snapped back to hear, *"Accept our gifts, our dance, our selves..."*

She stood with her aura fully open, like a Beltane offering, and the largest faerie homed in on my singing babe.

Before her voice died away I'd skimmed the grass, leaping and landing by the fire in a split second. I wrenched at my wren bag and crashed my hipflask into the fire. The big bad faery whipped round, snarling, and not nearly so pretty now he wasn't concentrating on his appearance. As his talons extended wickedly, the spirits from the flask ignited with a whoop. A ten foot spear of flame leapt into the air and nearly cremated him and I jumped due west to the babe and flung her to the ground.

There was mayhem.

The fire blazed to the furthermost tips of its being - and given its size, it was lighting up the field like the burning of Atlanta in 'Gone with the Wind'. The fair folk, rapidly being transformed into their real shapes, were haring for the cover of the wood: I could see in a split second the shining trail leading back through the trees to the rath. The campers were shaking themselves out of their enchantment, bewilderment in their eyes. The babe with the built, as Frank Sinatra puts it so charmingly in 'Pal Joey', had been shocked back into her body by the fall. Her aura, formerly drooping like 1950's knicker elastic, had snapped back nice and taut. And she was blazing. No time to admire the hawk-like eyes: they were boring a hole through me and she was just about to launch herself and do the job properly.

I sprang up and leapt for my life, back to the concealing darkness. Once out of the fire's ring of light, I saw her slow down her pursuit, hesitate and then go back to her friends, who were now squatting down on logs and upturned milk crates. Most were shaking their heads as if to clear them. A few had opened cigarette packets and I saw some interesting cigarettes being prepared: the very opposite, one would think, of what was needed after a genuinely mind-altering experience.

The atmosphere had been jerked back to normality by the shock of the fire, and I thought it best to leave them to it. They'd be safe enough tonight. I resettled my shades, resprayed with self-repellent for when I passed the fairy rath and took the badger path into the trees. I'd got a long night ahead of me, my hipflask contents had gone in a worthy cause and the birch dryad just might let me tap the sap....

Halfway there I changed my mind.

Maybe it was the look in the crooning doll's eye: maybe it was just instinct, but I knew that the night's activities weren't over. I sighed. That doll was a honey: her image was bright in my mind. She danced like a soft continent emerging from the grinding of tectonic plates below the surface, an enchanted landscape. She looked straight and strong: a match for a Druid gumshoe? Time would tell, dear reader time would tell. I'd withdraw, but I'd have to return.

The rodent activity had calmed down after the early evening socialising but the undergrowth was alive with the sound of nuts and seeds cracking, without even a momentary pause when the clattering wings the natural predators made themselves heard.

"Who, who, who?" Moaned an anorexic owl from the top of a pine tree. Who indeed? "How???" screeched a fox, more fur now than flab. I didn't need any other predator to ask me "Why?" I knew the questions. I'd give the camp time to settle and then I'd scout around until I got some answers.

5
Idyll in a bender

The moon had moved overhead by now: shadows were minimal and the fire had burnt down to a glittering bed of embers. A lone figure stood immobile by the far hedge. After a moment his arms described the time-honoured movements for re-zipping and he sauntered back to a canvas dome from which shone golden light. The silhouettes on its walls were like a Jan Pienkowski illustration: so peaceful. Perfect to snoop around, then. I strolled in to the outskirts of the camp - not even a psychic barrier to negotiate! I mean, even in Victorian England they used to beat the bounds: were these people totally clueless? I sensed the straight golden lights radiating from the central fire: without any barrier, that was what had attracted the faeries in the first place. I moved back to where I guessed the enclosing circle should have been.

I reached for the hipflask - hard liquor is as good for these barrier jobs as it is for wounds - then cursed as I remembered what had happened to it and picked up a smoking branch on the edge of the fire. That had been a good hipflask. Present from a grateful Odinist having trouble with her runes. It's only fringe perks that make this job worthwhile, as current mortal pay scales just seem to pass my boss by.

Mind you, sometimes there's a look in that wise yellow eye that makes me wonder... not that I'll ever dare to question him. "Butt me no butts," he'll twinkle, and you know you're a horn to a pipe away from being punted across the hedge into the next field. So it's an all-weather yurt and a small retainer for me. Could be worse: the venue is enchanted...

There, all done. I'd paced and smudged the circle –
purified it with the smoking branch - and the camp had
a modicum of protection; and I was outside the honey's
bender, one eye to a hole in the tarpaulin.

All women are best by candlelight... Remember Rita
Hayworth in Gilda? Change the waterfall of hair to an
ebony stream to swim in, dress her in Janis Joplin-type
tat and there you had it: glowing, golden, inviting and,
alarmingly not alone.

She seemed quite happy about that: liquid eyes and
raised chin; every muscle taut, leaning towards the -
presumably invited - guest. My heart sank and I leapt
back six feet before it had properly registered. The
leading faery: shall we call him Oberon? I think, as
useful shorthand, we shall. My mind worked as
frantically as my body as I wafted away the telltale
odour of smoke and rubbed my exposed skin with a
handful of dew-damp grass and leaves. Ten seconds to
think myself into a ragwort and I knew my disguise
would not be detected. I sidled back to my spyhole,
desperate for answers.

She had everything in place: all the elements with their
fairy attributes set out round the bender, a fae tarot
deck with the king card uppermost: this woman had
been invoking in a way that the others hadn't guessed
at and the result I saw clearly through the rent in the
canvas. She'd produced a full-blown etheric
manifestation: a fairy in human form, calmly raising a
goblet and toasting his hostess.
My eye fell on a bottle - cheap wine, so the label was
crude and easy to read. Good, that meant she was
providing the feast, so she was still safe. Believe what
they say about not tasting fairy food.

If you've forgotten, go back to 'Goblin Market'. It should be required reading. And, like that heroine, straight into enchantment, or rather enslavement, was where the chick was headed, I was sure.

As I watched, I saw them lean together, but where they should have touched, caressed, his body became amorphous and they drew back in frustration. Good. A real relationship would have complicated things considerably. She may be a full-marks fool, but this was a human being in danger, and I was the guy to extricate her. To hell with the primary objective. What were a few skinny predators compared to a human's soul? Yeah, yeah, very cynical - maybe I wouldn't have thought of shelving the first case for the duration if she'd looked like the loathly lady: I don't know, but I like to think so. I just saw that naïve babe and knew that she'd become my assignment.

While I watched, the fairy sort of surrounded her. It was as if his energy was doing an elaborate dance, making shapes which I realised I could interpret -as doubtless she could. There were promises there. There was an assignation, that's for sure. And, almost like a bee dancing, I watched him map out the way to the fairy fort for her. Looked like I was there in the nick of time. Once inside, she could be gone forever. I held my breath as the strange conversation continued. He was cool: he was mesmerizing. Whatever the hell hackles were, I felt mine rising. *The truth before the world*: that's another Druid thing. And what I was seeing was truth and innocence on one side, and black duplicity on the other. No judgment, mind: remember, the faeries just have different rules.

The candles burnt low as the arrangements were made, and then, with a last lingering, melding embrace, he was gone.

I crouched closer to the canvas: I'd doused myself with self-repellent again - any more and I'd feel myself become invisible, and it's pretty dangerous to overdose – but for now I felt safe outside whilst the visitor left. Only he didn't. I waited for the slight but unmistakable trail of glamour as he went homewards, but there was none. I realised with a shock that he must, like me, be hiding; but on the other side of the tent.

Now why would that be?

Cautiously I knelt to my spyhole again. Oh, no. Not content with messing with other dimensions and invoking those who were essentially alien to her species, having secret assignations with one of them and arranging a cosmic bunk-up chez faery, in the fortress of a faery stronghold, not ONLY all this, but she needs must put herself to bed with a charm or two, just to make her sleep the sweeter. And she was good. She'd removed the tarot deck and had substituted an animal oracle, casually leafing through as she sang to herself, curled up on a large bed, which, in other circumstances, I would have considered rather a wasted resource for just the one person.

I froze. Across from my spyhole, at an angle of 30 degrees, was another rent in the canvas. It was the perfect size for the dark, glowing eye catching the candlelight. An eye fixed on the woman. An eye which seemed, in my imagination, to be intimately connected to a raised faery eyebrow, elfin ears and a smiling mouth with licking lips. I was enraged. I mean, spying on a young girl. Were the fae totally bereft of decency?

As the irony of my righteous anger occurred to me, I realised the cause of the voyeur's excitement. Her voice had risen and she was shuffling the pack with more focus now, singing the while.

'Peace to us all, peace in the world,
The fox and the owl, the lords of the hunt
In safety the small ones will run in the forest,
May sharp teeth be muzzled and talons be blunt...'

The voice droned on: it was only one of about thirty verses, a bad sign in a young female: it looked like she might be too soulful for me? But, anyway, on the word 'blunt' I felt the shift and know what the faery had waited for. In some way, she'd fixed on a million-to-one gold-dust formula: if I had it I'd retire to a bespoke treehouse with hot and cold running squirrels tomorrow. She'd, all unbeknownst, made an effective bloody wish list. And had a sugar-daddy-fairy to fulfil her wishes!

Her wish had been for the animal kingdom to live in harmony; and the result had been that no predator had eaten since she started!

I'd seen enough. I lay back on the grass, gazing at the clear night sky. In the periphery of my vision I saw the glamour trail as the villain of the piece legged it home after a heavy seduction finished off with some mischievous wish-granting. You see what I mean about the fae? They mean no harm, but their agenda is... odd. Strange. And in opting to save the honey, I had unwittingly stumbled on the solution to the problem I'd been set to solve.

A quick rescue, show a grateful babe the error of her ways and undo the wish-spell to right the balance of nature, and Bob's your shaman: piece of cake. So, it does shine on the goodfella sometimes. Or that was the theory, anyway.

6
Snoops & spells

Half an hour later, she was asleep. How did I know? What are you implying, pray? Peeking in the line of duty is, well, a duty, obviously. Peeking because a nubile hippy might be sleeping commando...well, it might be tempting to a lesser man, but there are unspoken rules about that sort of thing. I'm a gumshoe, not a vegan-voyeur. So I had to imagine the soft curves hugged by the silky bedding, the languid grace of limbs stretching in sleep: fortunately the gentle pig-like snores were unmistakable. Unmistakable and, let me admit it, very touching: this babe might be getting under my skin. Then I remembered just what mischief she'd been engaging in to wear her out. Still, I allowed myself to imagine that murmuring breath gently puffing on my cheek, tickling my ear.... enough. I could almost feel the reproachful rustle of leaves from my birch dryad. I was on the case, and we don't mix business with pleasure. Well, not since that disastrous outcome - and, once again, I digress. Hmmm.

I rolled under the tarpaulin and found myself in the bender, warmed and scented by the recently extinguished candles. I sat until I knew that I hadn't disturbed her, and then lit my dark lantern for a quick shufti. The dame was neat: I didn't know quite what I was looking for, but it shouldn't be long before I found it, and I knew that I'd recognise it.

I inched over to the bed, careful not to look at the figure: humans are nearly as intuitive as birds that way, and as long as you keep out of direct eye contact, you'll probably not alarm them.

The bed was slightly raised and sticking into the middle of the circular space: from there I moved at a snail's pace round the entire circumference, though this is just a figure of speech, y'know? On the training course, advanced stalking of the suspect was actually tested by a stroll with a snail, which really taught me how things could be seriously difficult and yet monumentally boring at the same time. Longest two hours of my life...

Running my sensitised hand lightly over the possessions neatly stacked round the walls, there was a slight increase in heat that I reckoned was from a diary: should make interesting reading later.

I snuck it out and into a poacher's pocket, then scraped my knees raw on the ethnic carpet as I made the circuit. Past the entrance and three quarters round I was giving up hope when I was nearly knocked back by a blast hot as a Salamander's sneeze coming from a worn suede duffel bag. I put down the lantern and fumbled at the leather straps. The resistance showed me that she'd tried to safeguard the contents, and the figure in the bed stirred as I broke through the guarding spell.

I felt inside but a sharp pain made me withdraw my hand quickly.

My exclamation had disturbed her and those landscape curves were slowly shifting through ten thousand years of evolution under the duvet. Without waiting for the new terrain to emerge, I grabbed the bag and lantern and rolled back out under the canvas, wincing as the hot tin caught my wrist. Any deer watching would have admired my reflexes, and my ear at the tent wall told me that she was settling again.

The moon was still high and incredibly bright. The camp at rest emphasised the incredible deep peace of the slumbering landscape.

I fed the ashes of the fire until baby dragon-tongues licked out. The kindling was broken packing cases: ideal as long as you look out for the nails. The kettle in the ashes was pretty hot, and I put it back on to make a drink whilst I worked. If any one reading thinks that this constitutes taking the Michael, then I'd direct you to the ancient Irish laws of hospitality, which encourage generosity to the passing guest. You set up these camps, don't complain when we wandering visitors take our dues. Gods, but they were messy! I kicked aside a silver survival blanket and moved the debris of someone's meal - the usual odd cutlery & a salt canister. Placed that carefully now: the superstitions relating to salt have nothing to do with its expense and worth to the Roman soldiery: that was just a smokescreen. Really, it's often a tool for big magic.

My space arranged, I hunkered down onto a log. I left the bag for a moment. The cover of the diary shone silver in the moon and firelight as I slowly turned the pages. Bingo! Or, Gwychbwyll! as we Druids shout, especially when we've got a bet on the outcome of the Ynys Witrin championships...

Now, have you been keyed up with suspense? No. We both knew when I first touched it that it would be a magical diary, didn't we? Stick around me, kid: you're honing your deductive skills here: and you thought I was just telling you a yarn!

The diary started a lunar month before the camp, and this honey's preparation would have impressed an Edwardian ritual magician, and we all know how obsessive they were...

Yes, it was all here.

Three phases of the moon, blah, blah, purification period and letting go of obstacles... new moon preparation and setting her intent, blah...full moon invocation... every stage carefully noted, And a full account of her ritual as well! Ah, bless, she'd written it in Oldy-worldy script...

To contact the faeries...
In the dying moon, let distractions wane
So tread the path your goal to gain;
Set your intent by the new moon's light
As she does grow, so does your might,
To full of power when moon is round
Your spell will with success be crowned
And now begin...

Doggerel, admitted, but it did the business. That is the way it's done.

And underneath, the spell itself. To meet a faerie lover! The scene I was reading conjured vivid pictures in my mind, of Arcadia: the babe - Hestia, as I deduced from the front page of the diary - in her garden, naked under the full moon. The burning of herbs, the songs to entice the fae ones to listen, and then the spell, before she went inside to her enchanted sleep.

What? The spell? Are you mad? If I write that down, my next assignment will probably be tidying up after your mess. Believe me, you're well out of it. Bottom probably enjoyed his time with Titania, but we all know it could so easily have ended in tears. Think on.

So, mystery one solved.

The fairies were leaching off this little band of pilgrims like no tomorrow because Hestia had set it all up in advance, to try her hand at a little inter-species romancing: and the rest of the crew, seduced by the glamour of meeting other-worldly denizens, were happily going along for the ride.

Oh, dear.

7
Confrontation

Now, for mystery two. Down to the nitty-gritty of precisely how the predators in the wood had been disabled. Gingerly and with exquisite patience I unravelled the worn leather knot: I might as well have announced my intention with a conch call and fireworks. The moment the strings came loose, a wash of heat erupted and went straight as an arrow for Hestia's bender. Protecting and reflecting myself was an instinct, and in the nick of time. Hair flying, like a roe deer she was across the field and into the fire circle.

There my protection drew her up short and she flailed impotently, hissing and sinuous like a stoat. I tried to hide the book, but too late.

"What the hell... give that back. Now! No, don't hide it behind you, you bastard!"

"Bard, actually..." I countered. Inside, I might be quaking, but my sang had never looked froider.

"Uhh? You what???" She looked puzzled. I supposed that being woken by a magical blast and encountering an unknown smart-arse in possession of her most intimate musings might have flummoxed her a bit. Regretfully setting aside the chivalric impulse - for which the Dubh's are famous - to go easy on the poor girl, I jumped in like a fox on a diseased rabbit.

"Just what have you been up to, my girl?"

"Me? You thief! Your sort is scum. I recognise you: it was you who busted in here this evening, bringing havoc and then disappearing. I suppose you sneaked for some easy pickings and now you've been caught red-handed. What else have you taken?"

I felt the advantage shifting....

"Forget that, mate!" I shook the diary at her.

"You know what I've got here, and we both know what you've been doing."

"Her eyes narrowed meanly, like a weasel eyeing up a nest of fledglings, "What's in there is none of your business, so give it back, yeh?"

"And whose business is it? Have you told your friends - I mean the human ones - " she ignored my sneer, "That they're human guinea pigs?"

"What do you mean? You come along this evening, you know nothing!"

"I know that those faeries were vamping your mates whilst they distracted them with faery wonders. Now why would that be, do you know? I could almost see them shrinking as the faeries grew in strength."

"You sure as hell didn't see the same as me, then!"

"Of course, not! You were so busy with the big love scene that they could all have been vapourised before you'd notice."

She stopped at that, deflated, and drew a deep breath.

"What do you mean?"

"I think you've taken a wrong turning, and I think," gently, "that you ought to tell me just what you're doing." I saw here calming down. A gesture was needed. I held the diary out to her.

"Look, I don't know who you are..."

"Gwion Dubh, at your service: Druid gumshoe."

"What??? Now that is plain crazy! You must be a real fantasy merchant..." it's not an uncommon reaction. I gazed unblinkingly at her and she brought her attention back to the matter in hand. "I don't know why you've come, but... it's not like it looks."

"OK." I gestured to the logs and sat down. "Why not tell me all about it?"

She shrugged. I waited.

When she moved, I bent and poured the boiling water

into two cups, ready prepared. And settled down to hear the usual story: always the same yet always unique.

There'd been a bad love affair, of course: she'd been betrayed. Left disillusioned, she'd joined a group on the internet and soon she was into instant hocus-pocus. Have paperback, will experiment.

The other campers weren't into all that, but they were her friends. They'd all carried on to this camp after the Big Green Gathering & they were happy to go along with a nightly sing-song to meet the faeries: she'd got a bit of a reputation for making interesting things happen.

What she didn't tell them was that she was recruiting her new squeeze from the ranks of the fae.

What the faeries didn't tell her - and this is only my surmise from the performance that I'd witnessed - was that their energy had dwindled and that the contact was going to be milked for all it was worth to replenish their stocks.

Now just hold off on the judgment here: she approached them, remember. And have you seen how tired your old relatives get? I mean really old? Now quadruple their ages and replace their Bengers drink with a sip of nectar and dew. How desperate do you think they'd feel? And then along comes a gorgeous woman ripe for love and a group of walking energy fields: just what the fairy doctor ordered!

"It's the first night we've truly met them," Hestia was concluding. "That's what made your appearance all the more shocking. It was like going from - well, faeryland - into hell." Fire, booming noises, talons, teeth.... where did they come from, anyway?"

"They were already there, honey, in a different form. The shock made their glamour - their disguises - fall away."

"Then we weren't seeing the truth?"

At last the penny had dropped.

"You were seeing a truth: the one they wanted you to see. You think that Joe Pillock the cheating boyfriend was a con artist? He has nothing on the faery kingdom..." she bristled, probably remembering that I'd read her private thoughts, blah, blah, but I knew that I had her trust.

I refilled my cup from the kettle and prepared to fill her in with the old 'alien species' speech.

8
Regrouping

Oberon stirred. The rath was quiet and dark and most of its inhabitants had disappeared early behind the wicker screens that separated the circular space into cubicles.

Have you ever seen a cat take a pratfall and then saunter away, pretending not to be embarrassed? Likewise the fairy folk.

So, with careless ambling they'd returned, not meeting each other's eyes. They'd quaffed wine together for the look of the thing and retired, hanging cloaks and skins to guard their privacy, to sleep.

It's understandable, really. Humans might choose to live underground and call it ecologically sound and such a saving on the fuel bills, but we have a choice. When you've been driven into the hollow hills for your survival, it leaves scars, and saving face becomes very important. The other faeries were recovering with some alone time: Oberon had only just managed to get back before becoming catatonic. And now he stirred and examined the situation.

That night they'd been dealt a stunning blow to their collective ego. A major offensive to hold a group of Otherworlders in thrall had been scuppered at the last minute. By whom? he wondered, staring sightlessly in to the embers.

Fae memories are long. They'd have time to brood on this later, when they were missing the bright human energy that would have revivified the group: possibly the human servants who would have saved them the arduous toil of their long lives. For now, there was face-saving and he must plan fast if he was ever going to regain the respect of the fort.

And then there was the girl: how long had it been since he'd tasted the sweetness of a human lover? It was a time of ruffs and heavy clothes, he remembered: a love affair then was like laying siege...

This girl, this Hestia, who had contacted him so assiduously with her bidding spells and her offerings, was different, as the manners of this age were different, and he had found their flirtations delightful. And then it had all gone wrong.

His eyebrows met in a scowl and his fists clenched until the talons dug into his palms. He gazed at his forearms and hands. The skin was bark-like but not unattractive. As he concentrated, it gradually transformed, giving way to smooth, olive skin, the talons to nails. His immobility now had a different quality: it was pregnant, as if the body was just a repository for a questing, seeking predator.

The night was not yet over.

Damn! Freezing water from the standpipe spurted, as always, up my arm. I made my way back across the field with the full, soot-blackened kettle.

Ruefully I pretended to wring the loose sleeve of my robe out over Hestia's head. She responded playfully. Yes, we'd come that far in that short space of time. Charisma? Shamanic presence? Please, spare my blushes. She was alone: one of those souls who always feel alone in the crowd, and perhaps my otherness was attractive to her. Anyway, rapport had been established and I felt certain that she'd come round to my way of thinking. Which was? For relationships, inter-race was fine; inter-species was a no-no: *for the good of all beings*: that's another part of the Druid thing. Now, aren't you on a learning curve? I should market this as part of the national curriculum.

I spread the silver survival blanket on the packed earth round the fire and beckoned her down, so that we were sitting cosily, feet practically in the embers, leaning against a log. I prepared to broach the thorny subject of my primary objective: what the hell she'd been up to upset the food chain balance - as in taking a psychic mallet to break the bloody thing to bits?

Softly, softly... I built up the fire a bit for visibility and held the duffel bag up meaningfully. She looked sheepish and I fooled around breaking up more wood to give her time to collect her thoughts.

At the boundary hedge, the rabbit saw evisceration in the fae's eye, and fled. Oberon had left the sleeping fort and now prowled the camp perimeter: The weeds ducked to avoid his spittle and an unwary plantain shrivelled. He had transformed into a hunk – a teenager's dream: a boyband lead singer with attitude. Dark hair fell in quiff over a deep, liquid eye, but his staring, fixed expression reminded a spying squirrel of Nosferatu: a vampire in full seduction mode.

Again he paced, looking for a chink, keeping his distance from the burning protection of the invisible smudge barrier. He squatted down and sent his mind wandering to connect with the local wildlife... a connection was all he needed....

9
A honey repents

Hestia slowly emptied the bag. One by one, cards spilled out: hand painted this time, double size and beautifully done. They were tied with a hemp string and as she pulled the end of the bow, I felt a cool rustling breeze: she looked up sharply, a questioning look on her face. We both knew that whatever she'd done in the first place, her action now was starting to release it.

I held the first card up and the flickering light made the fox come alive - but its jaws were wide, obviously in mid-howl; the paint had run and blurred its feet as if it was stuck in the wire-like grasses. Hidden there, I could just discern small mammals running without fear...

I placed it underneath the thin deck of cards and looked at the next: a tawny owl, wings outstretched, with each feather bronzed with metallic paint. Its eyes were opaque, and mice ran fearlessly far below on the ground... a badger, with blurred mouth: a weasel, contorted... and below them, vibrant pictures of smaller mammals: plump, in groups, feeding, with come-hither looks in their eyes...

Whilst I'd been looking in disbelief she'd withdrawn and was messing around with the cups and kettle. I guessed that she was embarrassed: before I said a word, she'd been struck with the enormity of what she'd done.
"But..." I turned to face her, taking a cup of tea. "But...it's so cruel!"

"That's not how it was meant to be. I was doing some healing for the planet," I repressed a snort; show my true reaction and she'd close up like a clam. But honest to Goddess, it took all my self-control. Don't get me on to saving the planet. If we all disappeared tomorrow, the planet would actually do very well, thanks very much, and probably be glad to lose such meddling little ticks off her hide. This subject is less a hobbyhorse of mine and more a magical stallion of truth to ride the downs on a moonlight night. But the honey was still talking. I concentrated.

"I was working for harmony, you know," I nodded, assuming my best sympathetic expression, "And, well, if you look at the last card, it might explain: I'd been reading on the Western Mystery Tradition...." Oh, Gods, more patchwork experimenting. I turned to the last card. A large golden animal with solar flames round its head but a curiously benign expression, in a sort of yin-yang arrangement round a smaller, white fluffy animal. A small, pudgy toddler was holding onto the red leads attached to their collars.

I got it. The Western mystery tradition. Mystical Christianity. I looked at her questioningly.

"And the lion shall lay down with the lamb, and the little child shall lead them?"

She nodded, rather tearfully.

"It was just after - you know - " flicking her head towards the diary and the story of her betrayal. "I went out into nature and everything was so cruel - pigeon feathers in the park, a dead baby bird fallen from its nest, a squashed hedgehog. I was thrilled to see a rabbit close up on a grass verge, then I realised it was diseased, practically dead on its feet - it all came at once, you know? And I just thought -"

"That nature should be harmonious?" She nodded. "But it is, you know: you just apply the wrong sets of expectations to it. Have you walked in the woods after dark lately?"

"No: we've been at the campfire, inviting - you know."

"Well, if you had, you wouldn't have been able to move for rodents. And the predators are starving."

"Oh, no; that wasn't meant to happen." She was quiet for a few minutes, then looked straight at me. "I think I've been very foolish, here. I feel... ashamed. What can we do?"

I smiled at that trusting 'we'.

"You've started already, when you untied the deck of cards. Did you feel it?" I knew that she had but I wanted her to realise it.

A Cheshire cat smile appeared over Oberon's face as he watched the fox. Silently she paced the perimeter of the camp then, accomplished walker between the worlds, as are all foxes, she delicately felt for a weakness in the fabric of the protective circle and slipped through.

The faery pushed his hand into the invisible aperture, nearly clipping her tail. The air stung, but nothing he couldn't handle. He started sawing the air, and a shrill whine inaudible to the human ear sound caused the creatures of the subterranean ecosystem to shrink and burrow deeper. His hands began to smoke but he kept going, like a fisherman sawing a net with a rusty hacksaw...

10
The penny drops

"Oh!" Hestia's face crumpled and she dropped the card she was holding. Oh dear. Just as we were getting somewhere - cards being laid out round the fire, about to go for the pens and make the necessary alterations - and a fox had howled and guilt had struck, bigtime. I groaned, inwardly.

"Look babe, don't take it so hard. It's not your fault."

"What do you mean? Not my fault? You've just told me how it was. Who else can I blame?"

"Your, ehhh," how to put it tactfully? "Paramour?"

"What?"

"That great faery lover you -"

"Stupid! I know what paramour means! I mean, why blame him?"

"You don't think that what you did was sufficient to alter the whole balance of nature?"

"It wasn't?"

Give me strength! Innocent or arrogant? Bloody ignorant, I suppose. Still...

"Of course not. You went through the motions. You thought that you'd done a magic spell."

"And hadn't I?"

"Yes, of a sort. But you have to put a lot of umph behind it to really effect change." My tact gene working overtime, I didn't mention that the charge she could generate at present could probably be compared unfavourably to that of an AA battery about to give up the ghost.

"So what made it work?"

"Well, it stands to reason that that faery wanted things to go your way."

I almost saw a reminiscent smirk: may be I was being too soft on her? "So when he saw what you were up to, he..."

"Added the umph?"

"Precisely. By sheer coincidence you must have devised the spell so that it also added up to a faery wish-list. Gwychbwyll!" She looked blank, so her extensive reading had obviously not covered Druidry. We only attract the more discerning types, I've noticed. Fortunately she'd never seen it written, so we didn't have to do that pronunciation thing... I translated. "Bingo!"

"Bingo?"

"Bingo. Faery rules are strict. You've fulfilled the criteria, you get your wish. And those poor carnivores in the woods get fasting, for the foreseeable future."

"But he; Oberon," she had the grace to look sheepish, "Must have known the outcome?"

"Of course, but doesn't work like that. He's not human. He had a different agenda." I held her gaze and spoke slowly. " That's why magic can be not quite safe...."

Litotes: the classic art of understatement: very British. I left it to sink in whilst I went for the pens, a possible chant already floating through my head:

"One stroke, one claw: uphold the law...." oh, yes, I'd make a nice neat job of tidying this one up.

11
Spellfight at the hippie corral

Flash! I whipped my head under the tarp to see the air from the direction of the wood erupting into light that hurtled straight towards the campfire.

I leapt a guy rope, grabbed the skirts of my robe and raced for Hestia. Fool, fool fool! The trouble with the psychic barrier that I'd hastily erected was that it worked both ways. And I'd known that. And so we'd had no warning of his coming.

I was sick at heart as I ran. I admit it: I'd slipped up. Knowing the faery take on embarrassing cock-ups, I'd assumed they'd be out of action licking their wounds until tomorrow night. It looked like Oberon was made of sterner stuff. I saw the brilliant light pool around Hestia: and from it a figure emerged.

He hovered, just outside the circle of log seats, obviously wary of a repeat of the Molotov cocktail fire-effect of his earlier disaster. Totally focused on Hestia. I slowed gradually and stopped on the other side.

You've seen a still of Valentino in The Sheik? He was broad and handsome with the flickering firelight on his profile, and the haunting strains of faery music emanating from the wood certainly piled on the atmosphere. Think cheap gypsy waiter vamping a customer from any B movie of the 1950s, and you've got the picture. Trouble is, I don't think that Hestia had ever watched the black and whites, and she was buying it wholesale. A current of power had struck from him to her like an athame into a chalice. It was as if I'd disappeared, and I knew that he must be mesmerizing her...

I dived over the logs and grabbed at the salt canister left by the fire, swinging it round like I was broadcasting seeds. It described a wide circle, but too late for her - in that short time she'd already withdrawn to the other side of the logs and was pacing like a sleepwalker towards the wood as Oberon, a faery Svengali, controlled her movements. A spray of salt landed on her and he hissed and dropped her forearm, his hand momentarily changing to a twisted branch, but still she followed. Once at the woods, and she'd be lost.

But I was at home in the woods. Me Druid: you tree. Like Johnny Weissmuller in Tarzan, with a harem of lissom, leafy Janes – the dryads - to help me. I'd seen at a glance that evening that the wood was unhappy with the camp and all that was happening. The hedges were as threadbare as Mad Sweeney's robes where they'd been pillaged for firewood. The watcher trees on the wood's edge had withdrawn deep into their trunks. They looked like young acolytes drawn into those weird cults that give us all a bad name: as if they didn't quite know what was going to happen next, but could reckon it wouldn't be to their advantage. They were my hope now and they were some powerful allies.

I wrenched at the poor misused wren bag at my hip. The string snapped like a bird's leg on St Stephen's day. Scattering the contents, I dived on the Ogham sticks, the tree alphabet, each with its tree glyph, and fanned them like a deck of cards, pointing upwards and imagining the line they made arching over the two figures at the edge of the wood and down into the foliage. Now Ogham is very special to Druids: based on the qualities and powers of specific trees, it is *the* magic...

"....Tree and shrub alphabet, nature its lord,"
You get the picture? I was in tune and ready to go.

With a preliminary chant of the tree names in order, green rays flew between the sticks and trees, strengthening and thickening and lending the trees powers that their generally somnolent dryads hardly knew they could use. If only Oberon hadn't rent the psychic barrier I'd made I could have trapped him very neatly between this and the trees: the double force field might have whammied him back to never-never land nicely: but at least he'd stopped at the edge of the wood, and I had nearly reached them.

It was not a Kodak moment; not one for the paparazzi. Fortunately, it was only later did I realise the ridiculous figure I must have cut.

'My lords, ladies and gentlemennnnn: in the blue corner: the stunningly charismatic Lord of the Faery Fort, the culmination of a couple of hundred years of observing human cool. Tonight, resplendent in tight leather trousers and an Errol Flynn shirt; currently utilising his Svengali diploma of mesmerism.

And on my right... little Gwion, skirts kilted around his waist, Saxa salt canister stuck in belt, waving a handful of twigs with one hand whilst the other seems to be trailing - what is that, ladies and gentlemen? A silver space blanket???' Not a very even contest, you'd think.

But I knew had the advantage. My heart was pure. Those who've seen 'Up Pompeii' just leave it out with the sniggers. Yes, Hestia as a woman was as welcome a sight as the first snowdrop when you're planning your Imbolc spring rite, but my mission was higher.

 I was the guy in the white hat here - yes, yes, or robe – and I just had to make this work.

I swung the Ogham sticks in a lemniscate – that horizontal figure of eight of eternity - above my head, to get their attention: and I started the tree invocation, with the desperate intention of breaking the faery's hold on the honey.

My voice quavered:
'This is the Ogham, the Druid's own word,
Tree and shrub alphabet, nature its lord:
Carved on a stone or the stave of a yew,
Or written by twigs with the moon shining through.'

I'd got their attention now, all right. Oberon was scowling, his eyes gleaming like the phosphorescent fungal fairy lights in the boles of trees. His energy held Hestia motionless, but her head had turned in my direction.

As I sang the first tree, I could feel its dryad reaching out to me from the wood, strengthening my voice and enchanting the air, as if I stood in its sweet shade, rather than in the field...

'Beith is the birch, new beginnings will start
Clear all obstructions and nurture your art;'

The bright blessed birch cleared the atmosphere and I say Oberon's hold weaken...

'Luis protects and guards with rowan's skills
In peaceful retreat, keep safe from life's ills;'

Hestia shook her head as if to clear it, as if she'd discovered the Rowan's safe place within which hadn't yet been controlled and I sang with increasing power, moving to the music, drawing the glyphs as we used to write names with sparklers. And the green light followed the sticks, reflecting on the silver foil blanket at my feet.

'Nuin is the ash which links the three worlds
Study, communicate, focus your goals,'

The ash reached up to heaven, her roots deep in the earth: the invisible currents of the Lady of the Woods made a circuit with my singing and now Oberon, Hestia and I were encircled together and we were the three sides of a triangle:

'Fearn is the alder of bright blessed Bran
Intuitive voices guide creative plans,'

My mind was racing: that intuition can't just be whistled up and I was beginning to tire: where was this leading?

'Saille, moon-ruled willow, enchantment her gift
New currents are flowing and energy shifts,'

With a triumphant gesture, Oberon made a pass that had Hestia's eyes snapping back to gaze deep into his own – I was losing her. Note to self. Faeries latch on to words like 'enchantment'. *Do not use them.* I hurried on, a bit rattled now....

'Huarth the hawthorn liberates and empowers
Stimulation and change arrive with her flowers,'

The little hawthorns in the hedge really gave it their all, and at the third repetition, the change was happening, Hestia had turned and was taking a tentative step towards me. Oberon rose to his full height, arms upraised, curved, fingers like cruel claws, but he was no longer looking at her. Mad with frustration and inaction, he whirled three times to raise his power. Sweat broke out on my forehead and I frantically sucked in my diaphragm and emptied my lungs in a bellow:

'Duir is the oak, the doorway endures
May my will be done by a sacrifice borne!"

All in an instant, time slowed and I saw a beautiful girl sleepwalk towards me, and safety: I felt in me the power of the acorn, which can transform into a mighty tree to endure a thousand years. I was that tree, strong rooted, wide-spread and fully exposed to Oberon's wrath and I realised with tragic certainty that I was the sacrifice.

Oberon, like a 1960s mini in 'The Italian job' stopped on a sixpence and seared the air. A bolt of malevolence flew from his fingers to blast me to smithereens. I stopped, like a rabbit caught in a Grove's cresset flames, my robe folding like bark, and from a deep-rooted place, summoned my will.

My will was to win this, to ride into the sunset as the credits rolled; not to be blasted by a faery punk whose idea of enlivening the centuries was plotting the disintegration of the barriers between the worlds; a sludge-type stew with a bit of totty as a garnish.

The curse sped from his fingers, livid and green, and the instant before it struck I dived for the space blanket at my feet, rolled and flung myself back up, its reflective surface shielding my body.
Like an oak, I shivered to the roots as the blast struck, blinding me. The shock brought me to my knees.

It ricocheted off the silver surface and back along its trajectory, straight as Lugh's spear to Balor's eye, piercing and splitting Oberon, whose scream made a bell of the dome of the heavens.

Under its vibration I dropped the blanket and curled into the foetal position, all thoughts of Hestia lost, fused in vibration with the throb of the damp grass and beating air.

When the stars had stopped rocking in their courses, I cautiously raised my head like a lone survivor from The War of the Worlds. The air slowed and settled and I took a deep breath as the ringing in my ears subsided.

My eyes slowly scanned the edge of the wood. All was as before.

All except, slightly proud of the hedge, where Oberon had stood, there was now a stunted blackthorn, the victim of a lightening bolt.

12
Aftermath

A few yards away, the honey stirred. I stumbled over to help her, grasping her upper arm as she swayed to her feet. I followed her gaze down to my hand, and then held the other up to compare it.

Where the fingers had been exposed in holding the space blanket over me the flesh was puffy and burnt. As if I'd decorated myself for a Goth convention, every nail was pitch black.

We stood for a few moments immobile, leaning against each other, and then with one accord turned to the fire. As we shuffled the few yards back, she picked up the wren bag. I was so knackered that I let her. We passed the charred Ogham sticks, and with infinite tenderness I gathered them, my mighty warriors, crooning a dirge in their honour:

Beth, Luis, Nuin, Fearn and Saille,
Birch, Rowan, Ash, Alder and Willow.

Huath, Duir, Tinne, Coll and Quert sapling,
Hawthorn, Oak, Holly, Hazel and Apple.

Muin, Gort, Ngetal, Straif and Ruis shelter,
Vine, Ivy, Reed, Blackthorn and Elder.

Ailim, Onm, Ur, Eadaha, Iodho,
Silver Fir, Gorse, Heather, Aspen and Old Yew.

Hestia waited until I had finished. She stood straight and immobile to witness and honour my actions: she would make a good priestess one day.

We made it to the log ring and sank down gratefully.

"You did all that," shuddering and gesticulating towards the blasted thorn, "With those?"

I nodded, stood and broke them into the fire.

"But suppose it hadn't been enough? Suppose..."

My bravado was returning with the realisation that we were both still alive and unenchanted.

"No worries, baby. Didn't you hear the chant? I was only half way through my bag of tricks: if I'd got as far as the Yew, well, that is one serious mother to mess with."

No need for her to know that the yew is only approached after the blackthorn, the faery's totem tree. A miss is as good as a mile, as they say. And as my energy returned, I turned my mind to tidying up the rest of this mess - and then perhaps the stage would be clear for the after-show party?

"One more thing to do, ducks. We were interrupted before we could sort out that little spell you brought off..." my voice tailed off as I looked at the cards scattered around the fire. For the second time that night I fed the ashes to make more light, as Hestia gathered the deck and together we examined them. They were damp and soggy, and somehow transformed.

There was the fox, sharp teeth just glinting behind nearly closed jaws; the owl, his wings snowy white; the weasel, sucking at a rabbit's neck and the squirrel, leaning into a bird's nest to steal an egg. The rocky horror picture show to some, maybe, but to me it was a free champagne private viewing of the most significant masterpieces in recent history.

"But how? Is it because," she hesitated, "Oberon is dead?"

I thoughtfully smoothed the card I held with my puffy fingertips. A small cut stung with the contact and I winced. Grains of salt.

"Maybe, honey: that's got to be part of it. Though I wouldn't be so sure that his transformation is a permanent state. But when I made a magic circle of the salt, some of it must have landed on the cards, and look," I pointed to a tea mug on its side, "That's what dowsed them. Tea dissolving the salt, and making a good solution: the most purifying thing you can use. Combine that with ...that," the thorn trembled in the breeze as testing its roots at my gesture, "And I'd say you'd have a pretty effective counter spell."

Her eyes lit up. "And how will we know that it's worked?"
Oh, we'll know soon enough. In fact, I'm going to go and check right now."
"Now? But you're out on your feet! All you're fit for is..."
"Mmm, bed: I agree." I smiled and she blushed. It was a nice blush. Even in the colourless light of dawn, I could have matched it on a paint chart, it seemed so familiar.
"I mean, we've been up all night, and you've sorted out this whole mess. God knows what would have happened without you." a quick glance at the stunted thorn tree, and a shudder. "The least I can offer is a good day's sleep. Come to the bender." She rose, holding out her hand. I took it, wincing slightly as she gripped too hard, and let her pull me to my feet.

"Just a moment now," I stood over the fire and made my second offering of the night: the soggy deck of cards flumped into its heart with a whiff of ash and lay there sullenly before curling and shrivelling. We watched until the charred edges burst into flame and were consumed. As the flames died, the air stilled: the quiet grew from the jewel heart of the fire. Something that was a silent presence pulled our heads in the direction of the wood.

A gleaming white ghost coasted between the trees, through the dawn gloaming. Blodeuwedd: flowerface: the snowy owl.

Once again soundless.

We watched as she stooped and then flew back to a tree, imagining the furry scrap held securely in her beak. The earth let out its breath in a long sigh. Order was restored.

Hestia's face was shining. "You see?" she breathed. "No need to check any further, I reckon; you've really done it. Gods, I'm tired! Can we sleep now?" She was a sight for sore eyes, body stretching unselfconsciously: foothills and downs and valleys rhythmically stirring with her yawn. That bender seemed really tempting. I caught her unawares in mid-stretch and hugged her. Yes, she'd messed up, but she'd proved a good companion of the night. I told her so. She'd deserved it.

I sent her off to the bender, promising to follow in a few minutes, and strolled to the edge of the wood. I watched her safely disappear under the tarpaulin, and saw the canvas glow softly as she lit a candle in the lantern, then I ducked between the strands of barbed wire and made my way into the wood for the last time that night.

It was a mild dawning in the forest that never sleeps. Below the brightening clouds the deep wood held its secrets. But they were the right secrets; of nature in balance, without interference. I'd helped with that.

The air was rich with leaf mould and decay, crisp with the inspiration of leaves and bark. It was as restorative as a rich plum pudding and I filled my lungs.

Quietly past the sleeping fairy hawthorn: the loss of their leader should penetrate the faeries' dreams and lay them out for a good few days. Time enough for me to tidy up the hold they'd got on the campers tomorrow, or even the day after, I thought, as exhaustion began to fog my mind.

In the middle of the wood I found what I sought: a tiny, ancient Nemeton: the Sacred Grove, residence of the Genius Loci, the spirit of the wood. Middle management to the big boss, if you like. We'll draw a veil over what I did there, and not only because most of what I remember was the earth rising to cushion my fall as I fell on a pillow of leaf litter and gave myself up to the forest. It's an odd exchange, but it beats the paperwork needed to tie up most jobs in Civvie Street. The job I'd done was graciously accepted. I knew that payment would be due. And the form it would take? Ah, I'm no wiser than you there.

I rose revived. The strength of sinewy honeysuckle, the endurance of thorn, the regeneration of yew and the rejuvenation of apples lent me strength. I strolled to the birch I'd met early in the evening, so long ago, and clambered up to sit astride the lowest branch - the nearest I could physically get to the dryad, unless she emerged completely.

The bark was warm and welcoming. I sensed that her sap was sweep and delicious, and her leaves caressed my face, although no breeze blew. With a deep sigh of content I fumbled for the re-knotted string of the old pochette and withdrew the bent yet still intact joint.

I felt the birch questing as the smoke rose and gave myself up to the moment, sharing with an ancient one, lost in green delight.

All too soon it ended: I felt the tree withdraw and carefully pinched out the end of the joint. Head swimming deliciously, I hugged the truck for safely as I climbed down and felt our connection. I stroked her bark lightly and promised to return soon. Trees aren't jealous. Why would they be? They have so much more time than us.

I set out to return to the bender and my human brothers; and just one sister whose acquaintance I'd be assiduously cultivating whilst I recovered from this little adventure. With a smile, I anticipated the warm, scented bender, which would swallow me up into delicious sleep before the rest of the camp was stirring for its first cuppa.

As I ducked back under the barbed wire, the sun streamed through a cloud in three glorious rays: the Awen, the Druid symbol of inspiration, blazing from the sky.

From deep within the wood, I thought I caught the liquid notes of a pipe on the breeze.

The Gwion Dubh Casebook:
The case of the blast from the past

Mystery blaze baffles boffins
Outraged locals demand answers

Police and forensics experts are still baffled as to the cause of the fire which gutted the top storey of a local tenement building two nights ago.

Fire chiefs reported that the blaze had started with a ferocity that suggested an explosion, but gas has now been ruled out as the culprit. A further anomaly is the containment of the blaze: adjoining houses in the vicinity were completely undamaged. Eye witness accounts of a mysterious, tornado-like funnel in the sky just before the fire have not been corroborated by meteorologists.

The investigation continues, but a spokesman said that the identification of three men who died in the blaze had proved inconclusive and is likely now to remain a mystery. Police are still appealing for information from members of the public which might aid this investigation.

'Safety at stake: demand for answers' - local comment and pictures, page 7.

1
The Shriek

In the forest which never sleeps, the heart of the deep
wood holds its secrets. But one lone druid has made it
his job to plumb them............

The shriek.
Oh, yes. That was the very beginning. And therefore, to
quote Maria, a.k.a Ms Julie Andrews in Sound of Music
nun-mode, a very good place to start.

It had been a quiet time at gumshoe central. Things had
been pretty stable and, whilst that's not exactly ideal for
a private investigator, I'd been ready for some serious
R&R after the last case.
If you missed the account of my battle with the faeries,
you've missed a treat. There's no time to go into all that
now, but to bring you up to speed with the action, I'd
rescued a misguided, magic-tinkering babe from an
aeon of servitude to faery in the hollow hills, blah de
blah de blah and happily for me, she'd shown her
gratitude in the time honoured fashion. We Celts can
still learn from the classics, in which, I'm happy to say,
it's axiomatic that the hero gets the babe. Think Perseus,
think Jason, think.... well, Gwion Dubh, Druid
Investigator, actually: at your service. And that's
pronounced 'Duv'. Yes, little Gwion - and his paramour
of course; snatched, as I say, from a fate worse than
death, to happily succumb to precisely that with me.
So, after the big fight I'd sent her on ahead and done a
serious mop-up on that job, and, believe me, there was
plenty of fall-out. Resetting the time/world parameters
back to what we laughingly accept as 'normal' was a
piece of cake for a seasoned operator, of course.

Dealing with a fort full of newly awakened faeries buzzing like hornets had taken considerably longer.

My sympathies had been with them, really. Imagine the scene: you retire for a bit of faery shut-eye having suffered a small defeat. Your last waking thoughts are with Scarlett O'Hara; 'Tomorrow is another day'. And then…you wake to find that your king's been beaten at magic by a druid gumshoe and a human meddler, his spell to overthrow the balance of nature has been nullified and when you go searching to console him, he's a wizened thorn, rooted on the edge of a wood, with a cheeky sparrow checking out his upper branches for next year's love nest.

That's pretty well it. It took over a month even with the co-operation of the oldest trees in the wood and I was still lucky to come away with just charred eyebrows and a singed robe. SO…. now that you're up to speed…

Hestia and I had met up afterwards as arranged and she'd tended to my wounds… In a de luxe tree house in Sussex, with hot and cold running nightingales, wall-to-wall fireflies and the occasional nightjar lullaby, for that special ambience.

And I know your next question: how did I find it?

Well, every autumn, a certain lady of the manor whom I'd helped on a ghost job a few years ago follows the sun, leaving the coast clear for a self-employed opportunistic druid. I'm working by economic principals dictated by an esoteric higher law, of course, which allows discreet advantage of the facilities to be taken with a clear conscience. And my rescued babe and I had mooned and spooned until the neighbouring cows came home but were scared to look up, for fear of what they might spot on the observation deck in the evenings of hurrying autumn, and into winter.

Cows are sensitive beasts and I've always had a good relationship with them, which is fortunate, or Hestia and I would have had to drink our tea black during our idyll. It's the horns, you see: they focus celestial energies, making the cow a pretty poky, powerful ally. All that bovine serenity and cud-chewing is a blind: each smooth-flanked beauty is a seething cauldron of power. You want some of that; do like I did, living in the field with the herd, tracking their movements and thoughts over a season from bulling to birth. Or you could just get the benefit they harness from the cosmos by collecting a few dry cowpats on your next country walk. Your garden will thank you.

So, there I was, twenty feet up in our inland crow's nest. Ten o'clock, wrapped in cashmere throws and thinking about turning in for an early night, when it came. Cutting through the clear, star-brilliant sky.
A shriek.
We both sat bolt upright. Not leapt up, you notice - not when a stumble could turn it into a hop, skip and lemming leap over the circular parapet that circled the tree trunk. Rigid, we faced the noise, which transformed instantaneously into movement and a screech owl having a good gloat after a rodent hors d'oeuvre.
Except that it wasn't just that, and we both knew it.
It's not good form to blow your own trumpet, but my spider-senses have been honed by years of study: you don't keep a job like druid private eye on looks, you know. And since her rescue from the fae, Hestia had been alternating our sessions of mutual appreciation with some serious esoteric study - and not that crappola mish-mash of patchwork gobbledygook that was responsible for the trouble her hero had had to rescue her from in the first place.

So we both felt the change.

How many owls had screeched since we set up our love nest? Hundreds, that's how many. But none like this. Sometimes it's an owl screech, or a mischievous boy scout who thinks that if he practices enough he can still be a hero of Mafeking.

Sometimes it's a message. From Blodeuwedd. Flowerface. The Lady.

You recognise it and you go. Inaction is not on the cards.

2
Messages on the wind

"You take the high road," Hestia hummed softly as we packed our goods. Only there a month, yet, unbelievably, the chattels were overflowing the backpacks. Druid rule one: Live lightly. How to do it? A lifetime's practice, my friend: and frequent moves help.

So what had the shriek done? Re-connected us to the outside world, that's what.

An idyll is only idyllic by its temporary nature, and the world was calling. Think Ossian in Tir na n'Og, think Celia Johnson in Brief Encounter; eventually, we have to return to reality. The wind, bringer of messages from the depths of the forest, freshened, and it was a cold wind: after the solstice, the coldest part of winter was approaching. Underneath the stones and leaf litter, slimy despoilers of nature might be lurking, and if the punks of the esoteric world were massing, I was the guy to tackle them.

I'd had the wake up call, just needed some clues to point me in the right direction.

Hestia threw over a pair of pyjamas: I blushed as I stuffed them into a knapsack. This little token for the solstice had been most welcome, tree houses being by their nature a bit breezy. But, by the Piper's Horns, pajamas; and in the classic tourist tartan, shortbread red! Exhibit them north of the border for instant destruction of your credibility. Packing them brought it home how long I'd been drifting on the love lagoon, lotus eating as the seasons turned. I'd never had such a long lay off since I'd set up in business, little Gwion with his book of tricks and his blackbird familiar.

I gave Hestia a worried glance: how should I play this now? The life of a gumshoe is a solitary one and the Big Boss had called me to my next case. Suppose she didn't understand that? Being a man, a temporary breathing space seemed in order: I exited smartly and stumbled down the 30 steps of the staircase spiralling round the tree's trunk.

At the bottom, I had a quick cuddle with my old friend, the lime tree. My little linden beauty: what a star! Giver of shelter, warmth and a superb wood for carving to mankind, the root of a hundred English place names, and my refuge since mid-autumn. My accommodation and landlady combined. Druids and trees: it goes very deep.

There was a suggestion tickling my ear in the rustle of her twigs, and I turned to face the trunk and hug it fully, feeling the presence of the dryad, mature, warm and welcoming, beneath the thin xylem? phloem? - I'm a druid, not a biologist - of the bark. Her sap had slowed and she was in dreaming mode, but we managed a sleepy exchange of thanks and good wishes. Hell, I'd arrived as the swallows left every year since the ghost job: she knew that I'd return.

That done, I strolled into the welcoming dark to water the vegetation. Where next? I wondered and idly orientated myself. I walked a half circle until I was directly under our seats on the verandah.

There we'd been facing west, until the screech had jerked our heads round to the left. I replicated the movement, staring out into the sky to see the Great Bear of the heavens gazing down at me.

From high above I heard Hestia's whistle, 'You take the high road, and I'll take the low road...' and a grin spread over my face.

Tartan pajamas, the pole star, and a Hibernian ballad.

Did I need a regiment of devils in skirts playing bagpipes to know that I was going to Scotland?

Still, a grouse would have been a better messenger than an owl, I thought, and a clump of thistles promptly tripped me for my cheek. Interaction between the life-forms is essential in my line of work and even the lowest weed is entitled to pull you up short if it suspects you're taking liberties or questioning what we call 'the perfect plan'. You know, the broad overview that we're not intelligent enough to understand. Criticising The Boss - even in your mind, as I had done - is definitely one for the rookies; I picked myself up, rubbed my smarting palm, bowed to the great bear of the starry heavens, the ursine deity twinkling above, and hot-footed back up to the love nest.

3
Splitsville

I looked round, amazed.

In ten minutes the place had transformed. All evidence of our stay was neatly stacked in two piles on the floor. The bed, its head the trunk of the tree, had been stripped and re-made and she'd even whisked round with the kooky little witches broom I'd surprised her with at Samhain – Hallowe'en. What a woman!

Without a word said, she'd separated our possessions and was just lifting her pack to make for the door, alone. My hard-boiled persona crumbled. Those magical lessons had really paid off. She not only recognised the call, but who it was for - and it's the easiest thing in the world to kid yourself that it's for you when you really want that to be true. I was impressed.

I rushed to help her lift the rucksack on to the bed, balancing it as she slipped her arms through the straps and taking advantage with an unashamedly sexist squeeze that turned into a full hug as she turned... you get the picture. One touching farewell later, we were stealing away from the darkened treehouse; the cattle were silhouettes and we waved goodbye to them and jumped into Hestia's old banger.

I extracted an owl-feather director from the wren pochette at the waist of my robe and suspended it from the rear view mirror; we opened both windows and were off down the dark country road. Despite the breeze, the feather hung dead still for most of the way. Whenever it veered to the left or right, Hestia took the next turning it indicated.

An hour later, she left me at the motorway services.

I was on my own.

I suppose this 'on my own' really needs a bit of explaining. In the druid world, of course, the phrase is nonsense: nature is always a sentient presence. And if you're used just to human contact you'd be surprised at how comforting a breeze, rustling leaves or the sight of a winged familiar on the horizon can be. But, devoid of human companionship for the foreseeable future, I stood in the car park and considered my options.

Scotland had been indicated beyond doubt - otherwise why was I picking thistle prickles out of my palm from earlier, when nettles were so much more common here?

Check one: the motorway was going north. (Obvious? Maybe. But never underestimate the predilection of the universe to give you a good pratfall. Always check is the motto written above every desk in every gumshoe punk's yurt, tipi, cabin or office.)

Check two: transport. Hmmm: a number of options here. Believe it or not, it is not beyond my scope to sort of disappear when necessary. Becoming invisible is major league stuff, involving a fair degree of energy and maintaining your focus, so not for your amateurs. It could be worthwhile, considering the distance I had to travel. You just have to be nippy sneaking into back seats when doors are opened, and pretty sure you can trust yourself not to sneeze, unless you want to precipitate a nasty accident when a driver thinks his car is haunted and loses control at 60+mph.

I must have looked pretty picturesque, leaning against a litterbin to support my rucksack, one hand rubbing my neck under the druid robe's hood as I eased the strain of the straps. Or maybe the signs were pleased with my quick response.

Either way, my reverie was interrupted by the solution to my problem. And the speed of the result impressed on me just how urgent the matter was.

I had to be north of the border. And yesterday would be good.

"That's an odd kilt you're wearing there; don't you know your tartan?"

A huge lorry driver came striding across the tarmac, the cafe lights staining his beard neon green, spinning a stick like a drum majorette on her first march out: like a Celtic Jolly Green Giant. I brushed my robe down, adjusted my shades and raised one eyebrow.

"I'm travelling incognito; secret mission."

"A spy going over the border to incite clan wars, is it? Some dastardly English plot no doubt?"

I hoisted a shoulder strap. "And if it was; would that get me a lift or a fist?"

He shrugged and grinned.

"If you want a lift up into the wilds, I reckon that's your business. It's just natural mischief that makes me enquire, boy. I like to feel out a fellow traveller."

In this crazy, mixed up job, you get a sixth sense for your helpers. We call it feeling sib. I felt it now.

"Want a lift?" I felt his hands on the rucksack straps and eased my arms out of them. He hefted it with one hand, and it looked like junior's plimsoll bag swung across his broad back.

"How far up are you going?"

"Well far north of the border, and I could do with the company for the journey -" This last shouted back from me over his shoulder, as he strode off heroically to the lorry park, still twirling the stick. I scuttled like a hedgehog trying to maintain its street cred. in the wake of a badger.

'BERTOLAK TRANSPORT' was airbrushed on the juggernaut, racing green and gleaming, a holly staff with brilliant berries stencilled on the paintwork. I leapt aboard as the engine roared.

And that was it. Not even time for a cup of tea. We'd met and were on the road within two minutes.

In that hectic time - running to keep up before my possessions disappeared into the night, trying to remember a confirmation chant to make sure this was the right lift - he'd raced me past the lorry parked next to us - black, with a Scottish thistle.

Before I'd clocked the weird smell that hit the back of my throat. A peculiar odour emanating from it.
Before I'd realised it was the smell of death.

After a fit of coughing I did up my seat belt.
"It was a bit ripe, back there, wasn't it? "
"What, my cab?" He bridled.
"No, the black one - what a stench!"
"Didn't notice. These lorry parks aren't Beltane bath houses, you know."
Instinct told me to button it.
The smell I was coughing out of my lungs was sweet and vegetable: I needed a drink and he indicated a screwtop bottle on the dash with a jerk of his chin. I picked it up; elderflower crush.
"Thanks".
"Mm? Oh yeah. I got a case from a driver at that last stop. A fair exchange, you might say."
I didn't ask what he'd half-inched from his load to swop for the drink. He was a big man, I'm a well-brought up lad and it's rude to be nosy.
"Oh, yeah, the Sassanach can't get enough of rural treats. Elderflower cordial: fruit wines. A few bottles,"

he winked, "might get broken in transit."

Fruit wines: from Scotland? I thought of the balmy south, where hedgerows drop their bounty into your basket at the right season.

"So some Jock's found it worth his while to make this stuff up there and pay for the transport?"

My voice was incredulous.

"Not a whole lot of industry up there - leastways, not industry they give you a P45 for. What with grants and initiatives, every Jack the Lad north of the wall is diversifying. And you can bet the transport's added to the price some Saxon or Angle'll pay for having authentic beverages on the shelves for when the tourists come in."

We laughed, conspiratorially, and the truck ate up the miles.

I looked at the label on the bottle. Black, white writing and a thistle logo. Just like the lorry I'd noticed. Fizzy drinks and decay...I needed some space to get my head around this one.

My robe shielded my head from the shaking of the window as I leaned against it and relaxed.

Surreptitiously I palmed a warning pentacle in the cuff of my sleeve and settled down to doze. Yes, he felt sib, but even I can be mistaken. Check, check and check again should be written over every private eye's desk. If the driver's aura changed in any way, the pentacle would wake me.

His eyes hadn't left the road, but I had the uneasy feeling he'd noticed.

I shrugged my shoulders extra-casually and determined to keep awake, but the hypnotic motion turned into the sway of Hestia's hips as she rounded the altar, and soon I was away on waves of drowsiness to the nearest I'll get to The Summerlands in this incarnation...

4
Punks and a post-prandial punchup

I was out for the count as if I'd been slugged by a Cornish piskie - one little mother you don't want to tangle with. You know about referring to the faery kingdoms by the law of opposites? Hence the name 'the fair folk'? So you'll realise that the epithet 'good-luck' attached to the piskie indicates one bad hombre.

My head ached like I'd been the butt of some etheric pounding too. So I'd missed Scotch corner, Darlington, Durham and hadn't stirred when the wings of the Angel of the North wafted us up to The Wall. Dawn was a lady in grey when I woke, with the lorry heading towards a transport cafe and the driver leaning back and stretching as we came to a halt.

My brain felt fried. I'd had rotgut, moonshine and once some genuine poteen, but this felt different. Some drug, maybe? I picked up the bottle I'd emptied.

"Hey, Mac, is there any alcohol in this stuff?"

"No - and it's Bert if you don't mind, not Mac. It's just juice & sugar - you can read the label. Why, you got a headache?"

We were standing in the car park and he was suddenly looking at me in an intense way.

Like I was a something lying on a petrie dish in a lab that was just beginning to squirm, and he was an eager young scientist about to make a breakthrough.

I stilled. I felt no danger, and there hadn't been so much as a prickle from the pentacle still in my hand, but there was a new dimension to what was happening. I decided to challenge him; to put my cards on the table. Honesty was the best option. For a private eye, it was a refreshing and unusual choice to make.

Or that was the intention. Suddenly, the buzzing of bees on St John's day became a thunderous vibration that whipped up the gravel at our feet in a stinging spray. Five black motorbikes like summoned demons slewed at top speed into the car park, circling us before they screeched to a halt in one corner. Bert's hair was a nimbus of energy, as if raised by their wind. His green eyes glared and I was aware of muscles bunching under his soiled Tee shirt. His breath hissed like sleet striking a tarpaulin, and then he relaxed visibly and slung an arm like a small tree branch round my shoulders, turning me sharply in the direction of the cafe.

"Come on, Gwion; I'll buy you a butty."

Inside, by windows running with condensation, we got down to an early breakfast. As we were served, the bikers entered and took their mugs to the end with the jukebox. Soon Metallica was thundering out. Under cover of the noise, we started talking again.

"Do you know those blokes?"

Bert sneered.

"Scum, that lot. I see them a lot on the road; they often hang out around Hautdesert Ford, where I live. Black Knights they're called - huh! Always out after trouble. Think they own the road. Leave well alone, I say. Not a nice reception committee as you cross the border."

I dipped my shades and looked over them at him. Druid savvy told me that their corralling movement had been for Bert's benefit, not mine. Still, I was with him, and they were staring hard enough across the room to make sure they'd know my face again. Bert ostentatiously picked up a newspaper as they pushed past our table: just not quite touching, you know, until the last one seemed to lose his balance a bit and the juddering table sent a wash of tea down my robe. Very 'The Wild One'. Picture Marlon Brando in a kilt. That famous phrase sprang into my mind:

"What are you rebelling against, Johnnie?"

"Whadda ya got?"

But this guy was definitely a sub-Marlon punk, and I wasn't a '50s waitress. Impressed I was not.

I grabbed the mug as the punk grabbed the table to steady it, and snarled into my face, with mock concern and an accent you could chainsaw shortbread with,

"Sorry, Joe. Don't let it spoil ya holidays, now".

He paced out so leisurely that the swinging door nearly clipped his heels. Like his rodent mates, he hunkered down against the wind, fists deep in the pockets of his leather jacket. Bloody little bodach. "Black Knights' was blazoned on the back. Their kilts were identical, and no plaid that I'd ever seen, the background a curious hue of black that shrieked 'filth', offsetting the traditional cross-check of dull woody nightshade purple and livid pond-slime green - with no disrespect meant to the algae. The good ladies of Argyll must have been busy all winter knitting their socks, stretching high above their bike boots and each with its sgian dubh tucked into the ribbing.

I sent out a small wish that my antagonist would burn a hole in his on a hot exhaust. I was a stranger here, but there's always a friend in the landscape somewhere who might hear you; the North wind does a pretty good job of running ahead with news of new arrivals and most of the vegetable kingdom will give you a good welcome.

Sometimes the winds will take against you, of course; and that is one bad deal; avoid it at all costs, or reap the consequences. Think of the Midlands over the past forty years: the Birmingham typhoon; The Dudley earthquake in 2002; the Moseley tornado. Some black magician in the Midlands has a hell of an attitude there, and has royally pissed off an Elemental Lord. From the timescale, the left-path magician is A) now getting on in years and b) one mother of a slow learner. I digress, but you get my drift. Elements + respect equals safety. No good at maths, but I got that one nice and early. The winds of Math had been gently wafting us up the country and I was sure I'd be welcomed on my path, wherever it led.

Whilst I was putting the evil eye on kilt-man, Bert had got us two more teas, scalding hot to melt the fat coagulated on our palates.

"No rush now we've crossed the border. Let them get on their way. Now, where will I be dropping you off, ma wee Sassanach?"

A folded map appeared from a poacher's pocket in his coat, and we pored over it.

He pointed out his destination, and I made vague gestures to be interpreted as 'anywhere around there would be fine..."

I hadn't a clue where I was destined to go.

A fearful yell met us as we opened the cafe door. The air turned blue with biker-invective: my kilted bete noire was screaming with rage.

I saw that the gang had been hanging around in the car park with their bikes idling. Some of them were still scuffling playfully, obviously just time wasting. So I supposed that was how Marlon the Moron had been tussled up against his bike and held until he called pax. His thicko assailant hadn't noticed that the red-hot exhaust had had the effect for which I'd wished: a sore calf clearly visible through a huge hole burnt in his sock. I sent a quick thank you to the wish-fairy - actually a more malignant beastie than you might think, so courtesy's pretty important if she does wave her wand your way. We stopped on the way to the lorry to watch as Marlon tore himself free and ripped at the smouldering fabric of his sock.

If I'd known he had the brainpower to multitask I'd have been more careful, of course.

I estimated that to curse, jump on one leg and caress his burnt calf should have taken his whole attention.

He shouldn't have had anything left over to see me grinning hugely at the spectacle, but he did. It was obviously the last straw.

I was actor and spectator as time slowed.... with a hideous inevitability he leapt back onto his bike. Engine gunning, chain swinging, lasso-style, gravel spurting; he bore down on me like a maddened bull, and, through pure instinct, I leaped aside. In mid air, I saw, horrified, Bert on the step of the cab, body angled with his head inside, then my leap sent me slamming with my full weight into the half open door, sending it crashing into my friend.

A scream sent the rooks wheeling and circling above us, and Bert's body was hanging from the door, legs dangling, suspended from his shoulders by the sharp edge of the door. He began to crumple towards the ground as I fell away. With my weight removed, the door slowly gave up its victim.

A nerve-shrivelling screech of the chain scoring a valley through the cab's paintwork sent the rooks cawing again as I grabbed Bert from the asphalt.

As psycho McSock steered his black beast for the second assault, I heaved a deadweight half back into the cab.

There was blood oozing from Bert's neck and it looked very nasty. I dipped underneath the dangling legs and heaved again, shifting Bert into the cab, and pulled the door to after me, landing sprawled on the huge body.

A second screech set the saplings on the edge of the tarmac agitating, but as the mad one stopped the bike in a blinding storm of gravel to engage at close quarters, I saw the others lined up, and a series of grunts and honks from their horns set him racing back to them.

It was the oddest thing. As I peered through the cab window, I saw them lined up, a guard of honour from the dark side. A lorry swung into the car park, circled and drove out again with them as escort: a malignant goose swimming along the dark road with her convoy of gangrened goslings.

The van, like the black knights' jackets, like the label on the drink that had wiped me out so spectacularly, was black, with a thistle head of a poisonous purple and livid pond-slime green foliage.

5
Blood bond

The saplings breathed out; the atmosphere expanded and life returned to normal. I fell back from my position half covering Bert's body and out of the cab. Then I climbed, gingerly, onto the step, to see what damage he'd sustained. The red stains made my heart stand still. The Gods are older across the border: and blood has been currency for time immemorial.

To my relief, he'd started moaning and his hands were already at his neck. Not total decapitation then. I breathed my thanks to the red stag of the hills and a distant horn from a racing truck belled in answer like a challenge from the herd's leader in the rutting season. Red trickled through Bert's fingers. His green eyes flickered open, and a moment later he'd pushed me aside to make space for himself to sit up. I raced to the other side of the cab and jumped into the passenger seat.

"What - Goddess, what've you done to me?"

"Move your hands, Bert: let's see the damage...."

"No need boy, I'm OK."

"But the blood..."

"Ah, it'd take more than that to put me out of action," cautiously twisting his neck to and fro, grimacing the while.

"I thought I'd chopped your head off!"

A sly grin lit up the green eyes at the sight of my distress. They're funny like that north of the border.

"Well, maybe you did and maybe you didn't..."

Slowly he removed his hands to reveal a four inch cut, blood still oozing slowly, for all the world as if I'd been a clumsy executioner who'd had a practice swing.

"Let me clean that up." He knocked my hand away. "No need, boy, I heal quickly.

And I've got a nice little missus who'll do a better job than you when I get home. But...." and he switched the engine on, "I owe you one, OK? Blood's blood: it makes a bond. One day, I'll be after yours, I don't doubt, to make up for this. Let's just hope that we're still on the same side, eh?"

He gestured with a stained hand to his wound and grinned as if he was sharing a huge joke. I nodded, struck dumb for once. There are old and barbaric practices in Albanach, even so near the border, and blood, the life force, is held sacred. I huddled back into my seat, the effete southerner, and Bert appeared to put it all behind him.

"Now, we've got the whole of my glorious country to introduce you to. Can I offer you a night's rest before you go... wherever you're sent?" He looked at me quizzically.

"I looked down at my fingers, stained red with his blood. I remembered the stag belling. "Thanks, brother, but I do believe that I'm bound for the Red Glen. Can I just reach that map over?"

"No need. I know it well. It's just a caber's throw from my place, so you'll still be near those knight-scum. You take care, there, do you hear? It's lonely ground: you don't want to be caught there."

Lonely ground. Dreicht. Sorrowing.

Tragedies abound in the history of this abused land. What incident had given it its reputation? For me, it was a safe haven; my cousin had a bothy, well hidden from the gombeen man. Snug as a horsefly in a tourist's pie I'd be, and that was my destination.

An hour's ride later found me on the side of the road, Bert settling my pack for me, and a bear-like arm landed round my shoulders as he wished me safe travelling.

Jumping back in the van, he leaned across to the passenger window and threw out another bottle of cordial. I caught it and bowed thanks, ironically.

"It's a long way across the moor and thirsty walking."

"What? After the effect it's just had on me? I'm not touching this...

"Take it. You might be glad of it yet," he shouted above the revving engine.

As I moved from the civilised land of the verge through the hedge and onto the virgin soil of the wild, I heard him call after me; "And remember, we'll have a return match for this wound, brother!"

I turned, but the road was empty: just the echo of his huge laugh hung in the air.

6
Bothy Brother

The stars were out by the time I got there, after hours of relentlessly jolting over heather like a sword dancer practicing on a sprung mattress. My calf muscles were screaming. Dusk had fallen, and the colour leaching from the landscape had a strangely depressing and unnerving effect. Little beige moths had flown past me as I disturbed them in the loganberries, but whoever saw them in early spring?

I'd started chanting low, trying to tune to the right resonance to chime with the fey beings who were marking my progress. When I'd reached a passable imitation of Paul Robeson with laryngitis I'd felt the land beginning to respond, and ahead of me a line through the heather, thin as shining cheese wire, was leading me to my destination. I'd raised my pitch a couple of tones in a paean of thanks for my acceptance, and kept time to it with the marching of my feet. Almost I'd heard the echo of pipes, Scottish pipes, and I'd stalked on with hands in my robe pockets, to stop them moving - losing concentration and swatting the little faeries buzzing constantly round my ears was definitely not an option. I shuddered at the thought of the incident that that might have provoked. The glen was big, and little Gwion very small, and far from his native soil.

Once arrived, of course, it was a different story. After the heart-stopping relief of smelling peat on the wind I was drawn irresistibly to the sunken door under the whin bush, and there the air stilled, and I was alone. I paused to wipe sweat from my brow - I was wet as a naiad after two lengths in the loch with Ol' Nessie - and to compose myself before knocking.

I think my cousin Ruari must have smelt me. I'm sure that his hand mirrored mine on the other side of the door and it was flung open before I could knock. And then I was over the threshold and scooped up by a kilted gnome, missing the two steps down entirely. He dumped me on horsehair sofa, so misshapen I half expected a protesting neigh from it. The hairy plaid covering prickled me even through my robe. Don't think that it's only in folk tales that they spin from nettles: together one summer we'd made miles of thread, and with nothing to do but spin, dye and weave - apart from his proper business, of course - I was sure I knew the blanket's provenance. I'd quite possibly be sleeping under it as well, I thought resignedly.

Memories of Hestia's cashmere blankets rose before my eyes, but I turned resolutely from them. This was the North, where life is lived close to the bone, and here I must stay.

And so the evening passed with us in front of Ruari's roaring fire, like woodcutters who've stumbled on a gingerbread house. Catching up took us nearly 'til dawn, with a brown jug passed between us to wet our throats for the conversation. I had my last few cases to report, and he'd been busy the last couple of years with the business.

And a girl, actually, to add interest. Turned out she appeared occasionally, very alluring; often heralded by a raven over the moor, and on those days when the heather tips take all the green from the light and lay it over the land. Then she would come riding, to visit and to lend a hand with the business, he said. I could tell that he was a bit smitten. She seemed to have him exactly where she wanted him.

And any girl who can have that effect visiting a man on a boneshaker bike and wearing wellies must be some hottie.

I resolved to find out more, but my head was slipping to the arm of the sofa and I knew that, for me, the night was over.

What's that? Ruari's business? Hush. Discretion is the better part of valour there, my fine reader. But the discerning might have noted the reference to that inconspicuous brown jug which had been passing from hand to hand, inspiring wilder talk and more intimate confidences as the level went down like Thor draining the sea from the horn of the frost giants. And might wonder at the clean grain taste above the hard native water, alchemically fused to produce the Scot's gift to the world: whisky! And might just speculate on whether the bloody British Customs and Excise had ever received a penny in taxes on said product... I smiled as I slept.

The next morning we were up early and he gave me a tour round the works, half a mile away from his concealed den. He turned regularly to ensure we weren't followed and I became extra vigilant. When I say half a mile, that would be by a regular route, but Ruari had many ways of getting there to ensure that no footpath was ever made by his regular use, so it was well over a mile that we walked that mist-shrouded morning.

It was beautifully hidden: a bothy whose roof was built out from a piece of high ground that slipped like a miniature cliff down to the stream: totally concealed from casual walkers. Instead of making a track that could be spotted, he'd concealed a ladder in a whin bush, and we entered like Siberian shamans, through a hole in the roof. Once in, there was a door in the opposite wall leading to the stream. I took a moment to get my bearings, snuffing the familiar smell.

7
At the still of the dawn

After a morning's work at the still, an Elizabethan alchemist's delight of worms, retorts, intoxicating fragrance and the slow drip, drip of spiritous liquor, we treated ourselves to a sample of the finished product. By the stream Ruari unwrapped a napkin of bread and cheese and we squatted beneath the thorn to eat. The water looked pure, with a brownish tinge from the peat run-off, but I had been caught that way before: a dead sheep half a mile upstream could play havoc with your internal equilibrium, and being caught short in the bracken for the next few days with those bloody horseflies persecuting me like Dominicans after Cathars did not appeal. I reached for my knapsack and unthinkingly passed over the bottle I found in it to Ruari, who was choking on a dry crust.

He took a deep swig, swallowed, and raised his head. I saw his expression change and at his snarl I ducked instinctively.

I was showered in glass splinters as the bottle shattered on a large stone by the side of the stream and bombarded with invective.

"What the hell... what are you trying to do to me, boy? Bringing that shit to my still!" he'd grabbed the loose front of my robe and was shaking it, his face inches from mine. "And who've you been hangin' around with, eh? Where you get that crap?"

He spat the taste out over my shoulder, more by luck than judgment. I reached down into the earth, felt its strength flow through my spine and swept my arms up in between his to crack down and break his hold - and perhaps his wrist.

He bellowed, his face suffused with blood, and thick eyebrows arched up to his horny brow line.

My movement finished with palms facing him, chest height, and there we stayed for the instant before I knew he would fly for my throat.

"Brrrrrinnng, brrrinnng, "

What?? Was there a bloody phone out on the moor?

There, on the slope above the stream had appeared a vision straight out of Woody Allen's A Midsummer Night's sex comedy. It was surreal like that: a Heath-Robinson bicycle contraption of wheels, spokes and limbs, silhouetted against the skyline as if she'd just flown in, thumb busy with her bicycle bell. Above the moor, a raven circled.

Then she was over the horizon, the sun making a nimbus of her hair and revealing the sturdy limbs through the thin cotton dress. Her wellingtoned shins stuck out as she freewheeled carelessly down the slope, bicycle bell ringing, to pull up short as she reached us, doing a wheelie like an adolescent hobbledehoy showing off. She was an enchantress, and I was not fooled by the impish smile and outlandish clothes. She shimmered with class. She looked like upper management and that rusty bike could have been a prancing stallion. She was giving me the big check-out, and I wasn't sure how I was measuring up.

I saw Ruari's fists unclench and he smoothed his horns of hair flat on his skull. Fair enough. I shook my hands from the wrists as I lowered them. Unexpectedly, I had a breathing space to find out what the hell was going on.

"Hello, there, missus; would you be leading the Excise man to my door on your contraption?

"Not me, Stag o' the Glen," she replied easily.

I listened impartially. It's a druid thing. No judgment.

But it took an effort. I mean, "Stag o' the Glen!" Were these people living their own private Golden-Age fantasy or what? Romantic is not the word - but it would do: just spell it in capitals, for effect. Stag, indeed. Hmmmm. Mind you, I watched as Ruari's hair, in silhouette, raised itself in spikes from its flattening, looking uncannily like fledgling antlers...

I looked at my cousin with new eyes as they talked easily. I remembered the bellow of the stag as I'd got out of Bert's cab: and that was another little mystery to add to my cousin's sudden psychosis. Bert the lorry driver: All smiles and instant kinship, yet I seemed to have a blood bond with him: blood that needed repaying, for pity's sake. As I thought of him, the mystery Tallulah on the bike flashed me a piercing glance. It seared my protection, raising the hairs on my arms: and Scotland suddenly seemed wild and dangerous. I involuntarily looked at my feet, willing the little gorse, home of the fae who'd guided me the night before, to lend my effete southern body some of its tenacity.

Her eyes followed mine and then landed on the broken bottle. Face disfigured with disdain, she poked it with her toe.

"Ruari, I think you've got some explaining to do? This can't be left over from last time?" A soft tone: cream and silk. A voice to dream of, except for the razor wire menace behind the question.

And then they both turned to me.

She raised an eyebrow, threw the bike down carelessly and gestured to the hut. It was an invitation I couldn't refuse.

Well, they say that when you go back somewhere, it always appears smaller. Remember your old junior school? But I hadn't expected it to happen to the bothy in less than half and hour. The clean whisky fumes in the air caught the back of my throat. The fire looked sullen and resentful: as if I was now an interloper. The worm of the still gleamed, wickedly, and Ruari loomed over me as 'she whom I'd just had to obey' cut out the last gleam of daylight with a click of the latch. Roll over E. Allen Poe and Rider Haggard: these guys were taking over the crown of menace...

I thought quickly. The heather adhering to my shoe rose up in my mind and I invoked the clean tang of the moor, significantly lightening the air and winning me valuable time.

Coolly I walked to the fire, reinforcing the protective aura of the land, now pouring up from the beaten earth floor. I bent to the fire, presenting my back to Ruari, and stirred the peat into small flame. Then I turned with the universal gesture of friendship and amity.

Were they biting?

My cousin still loomed at me with one foot on the seat of the chair. Very handy for casually stroking his Skean Dubh, a wickedly sharp weapon nestling in the turn up of his long sock.

"Well? You've got some explaining to do, man. And you'd better make it snappy."

"Why? What the hell's happening here? Have you and your moll gone mental?"

She stiffened: I'd done myself no favours there, but I was past caring. Bloody Scotland. What was going on?

"I think, Mr..."

" No 'Mr': just Dubh, Gwion Dubh."

"....Hmmm, that we want you to explain why you've brought that double-damned devil's brew to this still. A peculiar elixir brewed by...peculiar people.... with whom we've had quite a history."

"Nearly did for my business, the bastards!"

"And as we know that, that... shite...." she wrinkled her nose at the word, disapprovingly, "Is only sold well south of the border, we wonder how you came to have any? And whether you've been in bad company?"

"And whether that bloody bottle will act as a sensor to bring the bloody psychopathic tribe who fence it down on our heads within the day? You pillock!"

I ignored the insult. Here was the trouble I'd been sent to sort. My assignment, at last: making head or tail of it could come later. But first, to the most pressing matter.

"OK. A psychic trail, that's my business. Cease stroking your weapon," he had the grace to look shamefaced and tucked his knife out of sight, "And get up that ladder and carve a circle for us to work in: use the stream as a boundary: they won't pick anything up over running water. Madam." I bowed ironically, "stir that fire properly. I've never got the hang of peat. And then use a smouldering brand to smudge this place. Then join me."

She reared like a startled horse at my tone and did the eyebrow trick again, but I'd turned my back. They needed help: let's hope they were ready for the kind I was able to give them.

8
Poteen pollution

I sat in the centre - one wobble would have upset the delicate apparatus, but a term of Celtic staff practice had done wonders for my balance - and waited for them to join me. We held hands. The woman invoked the land, I breathed for the wind, and Ruari, of course, had a quick chat with the fauna. His stag's bellow nearly knocked the raven out of the sky, and I thought that that was a good time to say that we'd done the business – by which I mean that the moor had absorbed us and no one would be led by the trail of that wicked little bottle.

I leaned back towards the protective circle, golden and strong. Now for the nitty gritty. Like what the hell was going on?
I felt completely at home - a nice change after the threats and mixed emotions of the last fifteen minutes. But ritual and trust go together like grannies and woodcutters. We felt like family: the Three Amigos, hopefully without the pratfalls. Pratfalls are bad news in my game, where you don't get to do a second take to get it right after the director shouts 'cut'. We'd adjourned to the easy chairs by the cobwebbed windows. I breathed in the whisky fumes, polished an apple on my robe sleeve and pointed to the lady first.
"OK, sister, what gives?"
"Sister is it? You might be changing your tune about that soon, stranger."
Ruari was turning purple and I shut her up quickly.
"OK; can it. There's enough mischief afoot without you mixing it. Ruari, you tell me. What's with the bottle of juice?"
"That filth!"

"Yes, I gather that it gets a strong reaction - now, cut the crap, cousin, and start telling me why."

Madam's eyebrow was up by her hairline again. I stared down Ruari like a Brujo facing off a spirit dog under the moonlight: time for him to dish the dirt.

"Well, it's a wee difficult to know where to start..."

"Just tell it like it is big R - it looks like he needs to know."

"Indeed. Well, I've had a nice little business here for a few years now." I nodded, remembering the runs I'd helped with, breathing in juniper smoke and listening to the drip, drip of liquor, with the air like wine and a full moon overhead.

"I've always kept myself to mysel' you know, but the merchandising has involved me in some.... community relations, you might say? And that's where the trouble started. I was in a car park waiting for a client, with 6 good stone jugs hidden under a tartan blanket. Well, no one showed, and I think now that it must have been a set up: I was about to leave when a biker arrived and ...made himself known to me."

It was my turn to raise my eyebrows. He wriggled.

"Loks, this is confidential stuff. There are, signs, words - you need to know who ya friends are. Well, he made the signs and tried to make a deal. I'd been let down, he could take the goods."

"Pretty standard?"

"Well, it felt OK at first. Then he said he was short of the readies, but his friends had a consignment of local wine they wanted to offload - ideal for me to process and make the spirit from, ye follow? Well, I told him that was no-go: I was known for the quality of ma spirits, all made from the finest local ingredients: no distilling off their rotgut under my banner; oh, no.... and then he pulled out his Excise warrant."

My poor cousin. I could see it all.

"So that was the deal. Do it, or get shopped: and this is ma livelihood we're talking about. Get caught once, and they're never off your trail. So they took ma stuff, and I took a consignment of Thistle wine, God rot them!"

"So you did what they suggested?"

"Didn't I try with the next run?" he started, when Madam hissed like a snake:

"Have you ever manhandled what you thought was a corpse?"

I looked blank. Ruari leaned forward and patted her hand.

"Don't take on, hen.... M' business partner," he nodded to her, "Found me the next morning."

"Green, he was. The colour of whey. And the smell in the bothy! I took him straight down to the infirmary - if ma bike hadn't had a crossbar to lean him over we'd never have made it."

My mind boggled at the picture. The resurgence of the Clan wars, forsooth! A sort of Hibernian amalgam of the Goodfellas meets the Famous Five. What goes on on these moors is nobody's business, I tell you. How unlike the home life in our own dear greenwood.

"And then?' I prompted.

Ruari leaned back and took a deep breath. "Then nothing."

"Nothing! A two day coma nothing!"

"Yes, well, we had to be discreet, you ken, and the medics couldn't find any reason for my condition, so when I came to, they discharged me and we came straight back here."

"To desolation." If Burne Jones had still needed a heroine to model for him, I'd have taken her number. God, these Celts do it well; she was the picture of tragedy!

"Yes, well, the fact is that whatever was in the wine had ruined the equipment. Rust, tar, deposit, fumes: it took us a week to clear the bothy out, bury what we'd found and then two months to refit the place: and tha's no easy by moonlight and starlight."

I looked blank.

"The excise men," she reminded me. Ah, yes. Those mealy mouths who mustn't get a sniff of the activity.

"So you two were working together for all that time? Hard work, but probably not without its rewards."

She bridled. "I'm a respectable married woman, I 'll have you know." Ruari grinned acknowledgement ruefully. "And this is a business arrangement: my husband paid for the refit - as it's on what you might all my land. " Her look dared me to ask, but I knew better. I'd seen the raven and heard her call the land half an hour earlier. I didn't need a diagram. Some folks can just do it, I've found. Don't know whether it's natural aptitude, heredity, a long link blood line like that chap round Cheddar: a blood line so long it went back to the Witch of Wookey Hole, I wouldn't be surprised. But anyway, these people connect. And she did. For the first time, I started thinking about her part in all this. And wondering about her mysterious hubby.

Rurai roused me from my reverie.

"No' all this wasn't so long ago, so when I saw yon cursed bottle, I'm afraid I rather lost ma plaid. I know you can't be anything to do with them."

"Got it in one, cousin. But I think I've been sent because of them. Wherever I turn they seem to be there, from my first pickup point in England to this bothy. But their game seems simple: sell this crappy rotgut - preferably down in England, for whatever reason."

They both nodded sagely. How many reasons did the Albanach need for wanting to poison the Sassanach?

Just read your history.

"But when they've got some left over, they offload it on a small businessman where they're sure there won't be any comeback. They get genuine Scots nectar in exchange for a lorry load of contaminated hooch surplus to requirements. All good business so far."

They nodded grimly again.

"So we're just left with one problem. If they're selling poison, how do we stop them?'

"No' quite."

"I'm sorry?"

I say that's no' quite our first problem."

"So the question would be?"

"How do you shut down an operation run by ghosts?"

9
Down to the nitty granitti

I popped the apple core in my mouth & chewed slowly. Yes, it's true about the cyanide in the pips, but, heh, perhaps I just needed the jijzzz to help me think that one through.

"Now I'll tell you, red cousin, just what's happened on the road that brought me here. OK? And then you can explain that last statement. A big mother of a trucker called Bert picked me up in England.." Madam snorted suddenly, but I took no notice.

"He was parked next to a black van with a thistle logo on that smelt..."

"Like death," cut in Rurai. For a sepulchral tone, my money's on the Scots every time. I nodded.

"Thing is, the driver had passed over some hooch - non-alcoholic this stuff - but it laid me out like henbane in absinthe. Felt I'd been seven rounds with the giant Palug Cat when I woke."

"Well, that's the stuff," Madam broke in. Except they do 'fine wines ' as well; with an even worse effect: but I've tried it on other people: you have to be pretty psychic to get it. To a trained occultist, it can be lethal."

"So most people wouldn't realise that it's poison? Interesting - but let's get back to your ghosties.

I saw the van again, by a transport cafe, with an entourage of bikers, with black jackets..."

"Those scum," muttered Ruari. Further description was obviously unnecessary.

"Now I find that they're behind a dodgy drinks business selling down south. But there's just one problem. That van was real. And McMoron and the other outriders that I met were definitely all too real. This is human stuff: not my province at all; and not one of them was a ghost, I'd stake my warrant."

I sat back, satisfied. Little clan wars and small business rivalries, what did that have to do with my boss? He'd rather kick up his heels in the Grove and go piping over the hills and far away, leaving us greedy punks to our own messes.

"Hmm," said curly-top. "Just to fill me in as well," her gaze was curiously intent, "Just what did happen when you met up in the car park?"

So I told her about the rumble, Bert's injury and the van which took all the psychos away. An interesting tale, I thought, but not particularly humorous. So why did she grin broadly and burst into an infuriating chuckle when I'd finished? Women; they may or may not be from Venus, but their thought patterns are definitely from somewhere way out of my orbit.

"You're missing something," said Ruari. "The men are real: all too real. The death-smell wagon is real. The poisonous crap they're selling at hugely inflated prices is real. So we're left with the question," he leaned forward, "Where does the bloody stuff come from?"

I whistled as he went on, "No raw ingredients, no plant, no equipment, no packaging or peripheral supplies, no depot."

"Just a van, six thugs and a huge, huge profit," the bird I'd named Greensleeves finished dreamily.

She knew that now we were down to the nitty-gritty, she could relax. Little Gwion was here, Druid Investigator; satisfaction guaranteed.

"So you think a druid will help with your problems; well..."

Her eyes snapped open.

"A druid? What the hell for? That's not what we need at all!"

I took a deep breath.

"But that's what I am, a druid investigator. And I appear to have been sent."

"Yes, yes," she interrupted. "But it's what else you are that interests us."

"What?"

"A druid's all very well for concluding the mystery: peace and justice 'n' all that," - airily dismissing my twenty years of training in the most exclusive college in Anglesey, "But we need a mystery solving: a mystery which isn't contained in the here and now. So we need the services of ..."

"An Ovate?" I supplied, as light dawned.

Now let's just fill you in a little here.

The Druid training is long, but it comes in three distinct halves, as we triplicity-obsessed students used to say. We were full of these little quips at the College, and pretended that such in-jokes made up for the long hours and lack of contact with the opposite sex. But, onto the training. Part the First, the Bardic Arts. Performance, poetry, creative expression; the brilliant bedrock to the training. Part the Third, Druidry; the art of being effective in the world as a peacekeeper and lover of justice. And that leaves Part the Second; that mysterious and murky territory of the Ovate. The diviner. The walker between worlds and between times. Where poky things happen and you'd sometimes rather they wouldn't.

Once qualified, all the gifts of the three grades were there to be shared. And Greensleeves had plumped for the Ovate package.

"So what can I do that you can't, mam?" I inquired mildly.

"Well, I'm in tune with the land," - understatement of

the year there. Chateleine, mistress, lady; any of the mytho-historical appellations would have been appropriate. This babe belonged on a tapestry with unicorns, and anyone who causes the greening of the heather as Ruari had noticed was some sort of a ruler.

"I've been over this land with my husband, and there is no trace of the set up which is producing that hooch."

Ruari broke in with a fond glance, "And if they haven't found it, then it's not there."

"Precisely. So, if it's not here now..."

I caught her drift.

"Then it must be here in some other *time*?"

"And we need an Ovate to travel the time dimensions to find out when."

We all sighed and relaxed. The peat in the fireplace hissed gently. Boiling water set the ill-fitting lid of the kettle to chiming and Ruari leaned over to make the tea. As if she'd just suggested a picnic in the park. Not an appointment with the Lords of the Time Dimensions. Women; all the same: get a mug to do their dirty work, and this time I was that mug.

The tray was handed round and we sipped thoughtfully. It was half an hour before anyone spoke again.

"OK, let's do this thing." I kicked the mug over. "Only I'll have to have backup, and strong back up at that."

Ruari straightened his spine until he'd stretched to his full extent.

"Yes, yes, you two – that goes without saying, but three is better for protection."

"The druid triangle?"

"Not especially druid. Most working groups like the figure three. The classic combination is compassion or love, power and wisdom. Ring yourself around with those and you could probably walk through Ragnorak taking Polaroids with no ill effects, but there are others. It depends on the propensities of the people.

"You mean like we just protected the bothy? With the land, the air, the flora/fauna?"

"Precisely. So whom else can you rope in to make the third whilst I go journeying?

Greensleeves also sat up straight. "That sounds like my old man," she said.

I was doubtful, but wary of saying so. Most broads have a blind spot when it comes to the hubby. He's theirs to belittle, but to the outside world they invest him with as much gallantry and skill as Pwyll in the land of Annwn. When he really resembles Mr Bean on a bad day...

I shelved that one for a moment.

"Whilst three people are guarding with - well, for simplicity, let's imagine a giant golden triangle," they nodded, "I'll be travelling; it'll be like browsing a gazetteer version of the Akashic Records for this area. If there's any activity, I'll find it."

"And you might solve another mystery at the same time," murmured Ruari.

"What's that?"

"The name of the Glen. Red, when there's no' a trace of red in the earth. Sorrowing, dreight, when there's no' one single legend of sorrow, or a history of battles or treachery."

Hm; interesting. Well, we'd have to wait and see what came out in the wash when little Gwion set the twintub of the dimensions shuddering into action. For now, I was bushed. It was only mid-afternoon, but that day I'd been up before dawn, trudged across the unaccustomed moor; suffered a near-attack; fended off varying power surges from a mysterious lady; set up protective barriers across a wide swathe of moor and been given a project which would make Iolo Morganwg sit up and think.

To paraphrase Tony Hancock, it was definitely time for my tea and biscuits.

I climbed the ladder: like a genie from a bottle, my head popped out to survey the moor.
Big mistake.

10
Preparation, preparation, preparation

A yelp escaped Greensleeves as I plummeted back down eight feet into the bothy, missing her by a goblin's whisker. I clapped her mouth shut with my hand and froze Ruari with a gesture; we stood rigid as the thrum of the motorbike shook the moor and sent pellets of earth skittering down from the lean-to roof. It hurtled towards the concealed bothy with the noise of the wild hunt in full cry, and we dived for the overhang, convinced that it would come through the roof. At the last minute the rider must have seen the concealed fall to the stream and the wheels screeched round.

Shaken, I pulled myself out and turned to see what had broken my fall. The code of the Dubh's ordinarily precludes diving onto strange females to the danger of their wind and limb, but instinct takes over at these times. Shamefacedly I extended a hand to the crumpled bundle of irate womanhood who'd cushioned my fall, but Ruari shouldered me roughly out of the way and helped her up, brushing down her clothing with a totally unnecessary degree of solicitude.

I rapped on the table to get their attention.

There was no sound of the bike returning, so I presumed the bothy's camouflage had not been detected. But it was a timely warning. The spell and Ruari's excellent camouflage had protected us, but we had no way to bar the black knights from the moor, and with the next foray they might stumble upon us by accident.

The time to act was now.

"OK, Ruari," I said. "You check that the coast is clear. Brighteyes, get on your boneshaker and go and fill your husband in on what's happening. I don't like working with unknown quantities, but speed is of the essence here. I'll have to take what's on offer." She smiled, strangely. "We'll meet back at midnight. Any black lodge worth its salt will be working around then, and far too busy to look out for us snooping."

Gently enough she extricated herself from Ruari's arm, which he seemed to have left around her by accident.
"O K, I'll bring back the old man with me," she answered, "And hopefully, you'll find him up to the job. I've never had any complaints," on which double entendre she swept out, before Ruari could check the moor. A moment later, we heard her bicycle bell. By the time we'd climbed the small cliff from the back door the moor was empty, but for a raven circling.
Two minutes later Ruari had disappeared into the heather, in search of my supplies and I was swinging in a hammock. The tendrils of the heather twined in my brain, dragging me down effortlessly to the depths. There was no one there to tell me if I snored.

I lay, huge, gigantic, a part of the skies, looking down on earth. Below I saw the earth boiling, and soon continents emerged... I pulled the protection of the Inner Order around me and relaxed into the dream...
Looking again, the sea rose and I saw Britain separated from the continent, the earth pulled like warm toffee and America screeched away from Scotland....
In a blink I'd zoomed in to the British Isles: ice covered the lands, and then gradually retreated, glaciers gouging out the great Scottish valleys. Before my astonished eyes, greenery re-emerged, and the first trees, the birches, covered the land.
I zoomed in again until I knew I was looking at this valley,

and woke in a cold sweat, tangled in my robes, my ears still ringing with a roar in my ears and above that, the sound of the birches screaming....

At twilight Ruari returned with food and we cleaned the shack. No, nothing magical like the Sorcerer's Apprentice. You have to ground yourself in the real world before this work, and that usually involves the scrubbing brush. As without, so within: purity isn't just a magical concept. As I scrabbled in a dark corner with a dustpan and brush, I wished, not for the first time, that I was some mystical guru who could get disciples to do the dirty work for me. Still, at least my robe was longer than the kilt. Ruari's knees were red raw by the time we'd removed every speck from the beaten earth floor. It gleaned dully after a token whisk with the mop - any more and we'd have been wading in mud. As it was, the draught funnelling from the door through to the roof hole was drying it in record time.

During sarnie time by the stream, Ruari put on his Man o' the Hills persona and gave me the idiot's guide to the topography. Pretty impressive too: dun-coloured moor and the occasional hillock were transformed before my eyes. Yeh, yeh, this should come naturally to a druid, but I'd been a bit bound up with the immediate action since I'd landed, you know: cut me some slack here.
As night began to fall, Greensleeves arrived.

"OK, brighteyes, where's your old man?"
"He's just coming, she said, don't fret yourself."
A bit snooty, and this was not the night for insubordination, but sometimes you have to ride the troops on a light rein. I let it go.

"Right, let's go ahead. You'll just have starlight to see by." I said no more than that. I knew we were all aware that it was the dark of the moon; a pretty poky time to deliberately go out to spy on the big bad. And it was in Scorpio; say no more. Well, the time had picked us, so we had to go with it.

"Now, the triangle: Greensleeves, you know all there is to know about this piece of land: you'll take the wisdom aspect." She bowed her head in acknowledgement. "Ruari, you'll take the love aspect," Rough, stag-like Ruari, my tender-hearted, gentle cousin: I ignored his surprised look. And that leaves only strength…"

A freakish figure emerged from the surrounding moor: hair wild and matted as the heather, limbs as sinewy as the tough whin and thorn. He seemed torn from the landscape, gigantic, leaning on a thick staff and brandishing a holly club.

"That'll be me then, he rumbled," walking down and half-lifting Greensleeves off of her feet with a casual one-armed hug. I saw Ruari sag slightly as she turned to us, beaming.

"Gwion, Ruari, I don't think you've met my old man?"

"Oh, yes, I have," I advanced with my hand out, to have it crushed in an enormous Caledonian mitt;

"Hello Bert."

He grinned and made a gesture of lifting his beard slightly; the last colour had long gone from the air but I knew if I peered I'd see a small but significant scar on his neck. Then he squatted and didn't move or speak again until we all took up our positions.

11
The show hits the road

Dreicht, the moor was. Sorrowing, lonesome.

Watching my companions walk away, dwarfed by its magnitude, being absorbed into the all-pervading gloom, gave me the pip, I don't mind confessing.

The awe-filled tingle between your shoulder blades as great trees press upon your back in the dark; the pressure of the sky squashing you flat on a mountain top; the edible thick dark miles beneath the crust of the earth when you lie like a fossil; these things I have known and survived. But for sheer deep depression sliding imperceptibly through your brain until it leaves you immobile, a Scottish moor's your man.

I distracted myself playing staring games with a little flower, smiling as the glimmering heather blinked first. Stop it, I suddenly thought: who knows whether I'll need its help later. Never antagonise the local flora. I moistened my fingers with spittle and caressed it's stalk: got no response, but I wasn't expecting any. The smaller the flower, the bigger the attitude, I've always found. Think Jimmy Cagney, with leaves.

I breathed in the surroundings and felt my mood lift. I was a druid; I was on the case, and zero hour approached. The earth began to hum...

The bones of the land
The blood of the sea
The breath of the sky:

The bones of the land
The blood of the sea
The breath of the sky:

The bones of the land
The blood of the sea
The breath of the sky:

…I felt my blood begin to beat through my body: a tide of energy that seemed too big for me to contain, if my fossil-huge bones hadn't supported the massive muscles and tree-root ligaments making up my frame. I paced my circle, feeling the energy from the earth rising to my knees, as if I was wading through water, and then I was breasting the flood, and then I was immobile, stretched between heaven and earth in a glowing column of light.

The far horizons echoed my work. From the West, Ruari sent a clear cable of pure orange streamed up to the sky. From the East, the Lady's wisdom ray of purple rose to join it, and the green of strength swung in from Bert a second later, all meeting at my central column of light, making the working triangle. There was an infinitesimal click and the door to the secrets of the moor swung open...

Crunch! A fist of power in my solar plexus doubled me over: strange air burned my nostrils and seared into my lungs. I felt my aura contract and steady, condensed in a thin, protective film. I levered myself up using my staff as a crutch, clutching my stomach, eyes streaming. Wiping them with the sleeve of my robe I looked out on a changed world.

The bones of the land, the blood of the sea, the breath of the sky; they were still my continuity, so I was still on earth, thank the Goddess: so the question was not, where, but when on earth was I?

Carefully filtering in the thin, rarified air over my tongue, I slowed turned, to find myself in the world of my dream.

Post Ice-Age, I guessed, with the glaciers receded and the earth greening; just like a scene from 10,000 years BC. All it needed was Ursula Andress to appear in a fur bikini, to the detriment of a gumshoe's blood pressure.

I was standing in the middle of dense birch coppice, with the sky through the black-lace branches streaming down aquamarine light to make my eyes start watering again.

Birch, first tree of the Ogham, symbol of new beginnings for Druids, from the way it is the first to colonise an area. It is a bright, delicate beauty, and with the most seductive dryads in the forest.

My horizons were truncated; this scene was bounded by the pyramid of power being maintained by the others. Towards Bert's green ray I heard noise, and kilted up my robe and went to explore. I reached the edge of the trees and stopped myself on the brink of disaster.

From green forest to hell, in one easy step.

12
Hellscape!

What should have been more birch forest had been razed, with a huge fire boiling a giant cauldron in the centre.

Semi-transparent figures flitted in anguish, stirring the boiling mass with great spoons, burning their pale garments, whilst others staggered from the trees, weighed down and cut by yokes of jagged wood, supporting buckets with which to feed the cauldron. Their fingers were long and black, like the lace-wing twigs, and green sap oozed from the cuts and weals on their backs. Goddess: they were birch dryads!

At the edge of the clearing, ranks of trees stretched. All had pegs banged into their trunks a couple of feet above the ground. With Druid-sense, I could hear the oozing of their life blood, through the pegs to the buckets. The sap was collected by the dryad slaves, to feed the giant cauldron. As it boiled, the syrup it produced would form the basis of that hells-drink that had bludgeoned me round the back of the head in Bert's lorry. From the horizon came a waft of death from trees which still stood, lifeless, drained dry. It was hideously macabre: a brittle forest, still on its feet. Dead but it couldn't lie down.

Hieronymus Botsch and Quentin Tarantino together couldn't have constructed a worse version of hell for a Druid: the total enslavement of a Forest Spirit. Better to chop down the trees and burn them than to enact this cruelty: only that wouldn't have had a value for the perverted crew who'd dreamed it up.

Here was the answer to our mystery and the heart of the thistle-logo firm of filth. A primeval forest destroyed to produce the raw material for an up-market drinks empire! I found I was laughing and sobbing and

and know I was on the edge of hysteria. Who'd be wicked enough to kill beauty and ravish our primeval past to service greed?

The cords of power at the angles of the triangle flared briefly and I knew that Greensleeves, Ruari and Bert had been rocked by my tide of emotion: if they were to maintain, I'd have to get myself under control.

OK then: whoever was behind this: I was now in front of them. I'd wipe the bastards out before they even knew I was there... I lowered my eyes from the sight of a fallen dryad cowering in a puddle of sap being whipped to her feet by some deformed homunculus, and gathered myself together.

The bones of the land, and the earth filled me again: *the blood of the sea,* and my blood coursed round my veins: *the breath of the sky* and I straightened up to take a lungful of thin sweet air: little Gwion was ready for action. And it was then that the blackness began.

I was caught on the hop, I don't mind telling you. Wren bag half open, about all set for an exposure spell of the big bad behind this. And when I'd found whoever it was, genies would have found their bottles spacious in comparison with Mr Big's new accommodation. When you see malevolent faces gazing out at you, seemingly entombed in the landscape, believe me, it is not always your imagination. Just walk past quickly is my advice.

And then, as I say, the darkness.

From beyond the pyramid of power that we'd formed, I could see a whirling vortex, as if caused by an oily chainsaw. It became a black tunnel and a foul wind funneled in to contort the slim trunks of the birches. Remember Briga-freaking-doon? Glorious technicolour, with hues you'll never see in the Highlands.

There, a magical village appeared in Scotland every hundred years... it was lovely, ancient, all plaid and coquettish maidens; very Gene Kelly. But I was seeing that magic in reverse. There was an eruption of the violent present into the sacred past I was viewing, and the thuggish bikers were in the clearing now, circling the terrified dryads, scooping up the deformed gang-leaders. Behind roared the huge black truck with the thistle logo: it screamed straight past, obviously on to another part of the operation, flanked by six outriders.

I scooped my bag and dived undercover in the same instant. The triangle of power had held: the bikers had torn through so fast that they hadn't noticed it. They were focused on the job in hand, which seemed to consist of gee-ing up the troops. And whereas modern management would have concentrated on personal development workshops and in-house training, these bozos had taken their strategies straight from the Attila the Hun manual of forced labour.

Peering through the sparse undergrowth, terrified of discovery, I saw the kilted, swaggering morons throwing their weight about: testing the reduced sap, holding sap syrup up to the light for clarity and letting it stream from the giant-sized wooden ladle into sticky puddles just for the hell of it. The slave-dryads were huddled at the edge of the grove, moving only when commanded; dragging their roots, hanging their foliage.

Behind the great cauldron I could see canisters of the syrup packed onto pallets, rough-hewn from birch: splinters and broken branches showed how crude the operation had been, and I guessed that the slave-dryads were the dispossessed, whose trees had been murdered. Cut of from the source, they faded quickly, so it looked as if the idea was to work them to death before they disappeared naturally. By the look of those acres of dead trees still standing, plenty of them had already.

Short of taking them all on singlehanded, there was nothing I could do there. I crawled on my belly to a safe space, and stopped for a minute, shaking with emotion and saw to my alarm that one cable of light forming my magical triangle was also shaking - the Green Ray. I couldn't contemplate what would happen if Bert lost it at this stage: would I be held in this place by the black knights? Would I be trapped by black magicians? The thrumming slowed and the green cable of light poured out, strong as before. I realised I'd been holding my breath. I crouched-ran in the vandal tracks of the black van; a psychic slime-trail on the land. Time to work out the scale of the operation, and every second wasted increased my chances of getting caught.

Behind a wooded bank a plank roof showed: I breasted the hill and extracted my hawk-eye from the wren bag. A nifty little number this: patented by a sorcerer who never had to work a day after his brainwave. It'll cost you, but this gizmo is magic. Oh, sorry; did you think that I meant a real hawk eye? Per-lease. I'll consider that on the day they plant real cat's eyes in the road.

Through the amber spyglass the scene leapt into focus. A huge barn, open on one side, so that the lorry could drive straight in and load up from a massive bottling plant. I kid you not! Here, in the primary woodland of these fair islands, a time warp containing a factory - and a factory run, like the plantation half a mile back, on slave labour. I focused on the production lines, using the hawk's sight to penetrate into the cavernous depths of the factory, then panning out to the back of the truck.

There was a sorry procession of nymphs and dryads, trunks breaking under the labour of loading up the black lorry with cases of poison hooch. And then I saw the impossible. In the background, peering from behind a wall of the barn, I saw Bert.

I ducked quickly, but not before he'd seen the glint of the hawk-eye. He knew someone was there. The triangle of power still held: so if Bert was now in on my action, not on duty as a watcher, who was holding the gate of the elements? I shelved the problem: after all, the magic was still working, and if we insisted on the right to know before we got on with things, then a mysterious force called electricity would remain untapped to this day...

No way was I going nearer to the factory. There were few black knights there, compared to the mass round the sugaring off plant in the clearing, but the odds were not in my favour. And a cautious private eye is the one who lives to fight another day. The fate of the foolhardy is left to the imagination of the victors, but, stuck in another dimension or croaking on a lily pad guarding a golden ball, the result's the same - one more of the good guys out of the action. And that wasn't going to happen to Gwion.

13
Planning...

I'd scrabbled back: popping my head above the skyline was definitely not on my agenda for survival. In a small snow-hare hollow I sorted my equipment: the ubiquitous hip flask; owl director; instant smudge; hawk-eye and, wrapped carefully, the Ogham sticks. Little slivers of tree-power, right under my hand. Shocked, I realised they were cold to the touch where they should have emanated warmth: half of these beauties – trees indigenous to the islands for hundreds of years - were bereft of power in this far-distant age, not having yet colonised after the ice floes had left. I dropped them in fright as a hand like a bear's paw thumped on my shoulder, pinning me in place.

"OK. Little Gwion, what's going on here?"

Two shocks together in such circumstances could be regarded as one too many. With a regrettable lapse in cool caused, I'm convinced, by my extrusion of my etheric double, I shrieked and grabbed the big clown's shirt instinctively.

"Bert, you bastard! I'll bloody swing for you. How did you get here?"

"Oh, stop belly-aching. You'd have known about it if I'd got your attention with this." He swung the holly club menacingly. I remembered our disparity in size, and backed off. "I just crawled round the back of yon factory as soon as I spotted you: good job the black knights were otherwise engaged."

I bristled. No one wants their professionalism impugned. But he still needed help, and he had his pride, so I let it go.

"Not how did you get round the corner! I mean, what are you doing..." gesturing helplessly around the primordial landscape, held by our magic and now violated by the black magician's entrance tunnel "...here? I mean, correct me if I'm wrong, but aren't you, to mis-quote Michael Caine, only supposed to keep the bloody power up?"

He waved his club at the shimmering horizon, through which we could both see the green line of power. "Alakazam! As we say in the trade. There she still blows."

"But how?"

"Ways and means, little son. But you'll notice there's something missing?"

I remembered his first appearance: bloody menacing as he appeared out of the heather with his club, and leaning on...

"Your staff?" I was disbelieving.

"Too true. When I felt the structure wobbling I thought you might need a bit of back up. I planted the staff to earth the power, and - job done!"

We left it there. Time was wasting. If I suspected that an ugly-mug outsize truck driver had powers that made him a major player, now was not the time to pursue it. He spat expressively.

"So what do you propose, Gwion boy?"

I'd never felt so hopeless. I gestured at my pitiful tools. I knew that there was a solution, but where was it?

Pulling the hood over my head, I withdrew a few yards. Never underestimate the effect of restricting your vision; the finest aid to focus that I've found. Which makes horses who habitually wear blinkers pretty sharp animals, in my experience. Through my half-closed eyes the glittering bark of a tender birch in the thin air caused light refractions: the whole scene telescoped until I could hold the landscape in my hand.

Scene one: a hell's kitchen producing hundreds of gallons of birch sap, killing the forests for miles around. Tracks from plugged trees where full buckets were trudged to the giant cauldron for the sugaring off, the boiling, condensing the sap to thick syrup.

Scene two: a tawdry factory, completing the process.

Backcloth: a butchered forest, being slowly bled dry.

And hundreds of innocent slave-dryads, forced into the destruction of their own habitat. A black lodge had forced a rent through the fabric of time to despoil the virgin landscape. I ground my teeth.

OK, Gwion, now we're getting somewhere.

There were two stages; to stop the operation, and then to sever the connection, forever. Limiting civilian – or dryad - casualties would be good, but this one was so big that that couldn't be my priority.

One thing was for certain: the tree-power which was my usual modus operandi wouldn't be any good for this one, with just one major tree species in existence, and that already in thrall to dark magic.

The roaring of the lorry's engine shifted me back into present time and Bert slid down the slope from his vantage point.

"We've got a few minutes yet. It's only half loaded, so the bastard's just revving his engine to stress out those poor workers: every lungful of that exhaust's making them go green in good and earnest. So, brother, time for the plan."

Like a flash, it came; the lightning flash of inspiration: the plan was there, in its entirety. We'd go back to beyond the trees; back to a more primal source of power.

"Use fire to fight fire: let's go!"

And before he could ask, I'd grabbed my gear and was half way round the incline, making for the back of the factory.

Goddess, but that big guy could move. I didn't feel him at my shoulder, but as I eased up against a rough timber support, there he was, club, questions and all.

"OK, and your plan would be..?"

"Situation: two of us: a lot of them - those black lodges love the stereotype bad stuff, so I'd guess thirteen. If they could live in a Dennis Wheatley film, they would. So, twelve goons on bikes and one lorry driver."

"That makes six and a half brace..." said Bert, dreamily.

"OK, OK, don't go all revenge of the glens on me, mate. Some might get injured, but I'm a private eye, not a hired assassin. We'll try to solve your problems my way, to start with."

"Well, you've got us here; that makes you the boss."

14
Draco rising

Clouds of black exhaust reached us, making the precious stones I pulled out of my bag gleam even more brightly, like otherworldly eyes: citrine, aquamarine, ruby and emerald. As they began to gather the light to themselves, Bert swore. He recognised them, and he slapped his hand over mine and between us we held their power: the four Dragon Stones of the Islands. In each one was stored a fragment of the energy-lines of the land. *The actual land.* Since before the Ice Age, the land had been shaped by the movements of these mythic beasts, and as protectors, it was their job to deal with this despoilation. If I got it right, that is.

The outlines of our fingers were glowing red and semi-transparent as if we held them out to a fire. I hoped that the thin factory wall would shield and hide us as we worked, but it was too late to worry as the power surged and a chant was ripped from me. Before the trees, at the beginning of time, what was there?

The bones of the land
The blood of the sea
The breath of the sky...

And the essence of the power of each, we pictured as a dragon...

My voice grated and shrieked like the crunching of rocks: it rattled like gravel in my throat...

Dragon of the Earth, hear as I
Chant through your chthonic caverns,
Along curving veins of copper, seams of coal

Into the core of your vastness.
By your mineral treasure, in defence of your violated
skin, awaken!

The earth heaved as if a great creature was waking.
Bert's shriek was far-off as the emerald burnt white-hot
and leapt from his hand to the ground.

Still in trance, I clawed it where it stuck to the earth like
a magnet and skimmed it. The air grew a surface like a
scaled wing: the stone bounced twice on it and
exploded with vegetable mass, with crystalline shards
that pierced the black knights and seared through
metal. Screaming and streaming with blood, they
erupted from the back of the truck and scattered.

I mewed like a buzzard, screamed like a condor...

Dragon of the air, hear me!
Pinions sweep above snow-tipped precipice,
Endlessly circling in the pure vastness,
In your soaring sovereignty of the sky.
By your piercing clarity and vision, your gift,
I awaken you!

I threw the citrine up high in the air and staggered,
falling to my knees as a great rushing wind funneled
like a huge air-borne body flying in from the east,
booming through the openings in the factory, a giant
knocking building blocks of pallets and stacked bottles.

The supports of the factory cracked like elven bones
and falling beams slammed the black knights. I felt a
knee braced behind me and pulled myself up, using
Bert as both lever and shield against flying debris.

I held the third stone aloft in the howling gale and faced into the wind. Of its own volition, my chest rose rhythmically like a long distance swimmer and my voice box boomed...

Dragon of water, hear me!
Ancient worm, suspended and weightless
In uncharted depths,
With the whale's call I sing to you,
With the susurration of the wash of the wave,
Deep in the giver of life you lurk; rise to my song!

I gazed round wildly: where would we find the water in this cold and pristine landscape?

An ear-splitting crack from the middle distance answered me.

I was thrown to the earth as the ground shook, and from beneath the glacier the creaking of leathery wings set the ice to splitting and grating as it ground against itself.

I threw the aquamarine in its direction with the force of a grenade and it hit the ice. Under the frozen skin a huge tongue licked and a split appeared from high up: top slush avalanched down, liquefying as it poured and plummeted into a flash flood carrying boulders to pulverise the factory and destroy all evidence of it.

Bert slung me over his shoulder and threw me into the back of the black van, clubbing all opposition out of the way, and there I lay, gasping and gagging on the smell from the shattered bottles, my robe protecting me frommost of the broken glass. I was lifted and slammed back into the van's side as it made 0-60 in the blink of a genie's eye.

We hit a bump which I suspected was the dislodged driver, and we hurtled out of the path of the water.

No sooner had I sat up and taken stock - there were four bedraggled dryads in there with me, weeping sap over the detritus - than we screeched to a halt, the half-door was let down and Bert was hauling us all out at the clearing.

The scene was indescribable. The fallout of dragon energy was spreading out, and the landscape was boiling and heaving. Spray from the moving glacier hung knee-high as fog, through which the staggering dryads waded in panic, their long toes sinking into the earth with each step to anchor them against the wind. A homunculus with a whip bowled through the mist like tumbleweed in a B western, and a black knight was heaving at a pile of mangled bikes. A group of bikers dragged their mate away from the pile and they started to round up the dryads, who'd all turned to see the torrent of water where a valley had been just seconds before. Titanic meets The Wild One, yeh!

The huge tripod over the fire lurched but held firm.

The McMoron clan was pushing the dryads practically into the fire in an attempt to stabilise the wildly-swinging cauldron. I grabbed one dryad and pulled her out of the path of a motorbike careering over earth that was heaving: beneath us, one mother of all moles was racing pell-mell through new tunnels. The magical funnel through which the bikers had driven their hell's cavalcade from the present world an aeon away was throbbing. I knew that on the other end, in our world, a group of dedicated black magicians had got wind of our activity. Time for Gwion and the good guy to act now, before they sent reinforcements.

The stench of smouldering tree-fibre was adding to the mist through which we all waded, thigh deep. The roaring of the cataract filled the air.

I began to feel most peculiar.

15
Going for the burn

The ruby burnt my hand, and I glanced around. Earth, Air, Water: what had happened to the fourth dragon? The air was alive with psychic wingbeats powering the flood, the mist, upheaving the earth. Where was the Fire?

A deep roar filled the air; my throat distended to let it out in a wave of searing vapour as the ruby burnt through my palm. Deep inside me, agonising heat exploded as a red-hot serpent uncoiling along the length of my spine until I felt my brain would fry. Wildly I thrashed to dissipate the heat. The dryad seemed locked onto my hand as if by electricity, and when she snapped her arm free, I saw the blackened stump through glazing eyes.

My arms raised like mighty wings, but the heat and the pressure building up inside me made my knees buckle, and Bert, faithful Bert, grabbed me round the waist and turned us both to the black tunnel.

The remaining black knights were grouped around the opening and their chanting added another dimension to our Hell's Kitchen. With each raucous bellow, a stench emanated from the tunnel: at its core, we could see a pool of the darkness of decay: a rancid, oily, filthy nothingness which was approaching the violated land, drawn by the fiend's chorus and the clanking of their bike chains.

My triangle of power trembled as if it sensed the imminent onslaught of bile-curdling evil, and Bert, his clothing singeing and smouldering where he touched me, pointed me at the tunnel and ran. Like a human battering ram at a medieval castle gate, he propelled me toward the coven ritual.

And, seeing myself bound for certain death, I relaxed and let whatever was inside me, use me.

My arms stretched out straight; the cracking of my joints and ligaments was like the crackling of a fire, and - rather late in the day, I afterwards thought - the invocation came....

Dragon of the fire, hear me!
Salamander-smooth, ardent asbestos body;
heat maker, cauldron boiler
Spirit-purifier of our race,

The sweat was pouring from my body; Bert had covered half the distance and the coven were swinging chains threateningly; biding their time; waiting.

Awaken and avenge the ravaged earth,
Cleanse the miasma from its face:
Passion for the earth, use me now...

Whatever they saw as we ran on them, the coven were struggling to get away now, terror on their faces, but the heather, my darling little ling, had entwined round their ankles and they were helpless. They crouched defensively as we approached.

With a searing belch a torrent of flame issued from my mouth, straight past the black acolytes and into the magical tunnel, writhing with the core of rottenness and corruption and blasting it into an inferno. A putrid and foetid cloud hung round the entrance and dropped the remaining knights in their tracks.
My fiery breath raced further up to the source, until the black vortex was a living tunnel of iridescent flame, rolling curtains of fire of every hue, and I flew free of

my body and travelled within, on wings of molten metal.

Through my dragon-hooded eyes I glimpsed a dingy, high- ceilinged room. Its black candles revealed a huddled animal corpse, smelling rancid, and dark staining on the painted floorboards. Men cowered as I appeared in the corner; the leader, his credentials on the line, grabbed a chalice and flung its oily, viscous contents at me. They evaporated as I breathed fire into the room. As the curtains caught and melted with a stink and oily smoke, I stretched my brazen wings and felt the paper-thin walls buckling.

My human mind reasserted itself and I called back to Bert, to pull me out of there, but there was no response. Again and again I roared, my scaly neck rotating like a snake's as I searched for the psychic tunnel through which I'd arrived. My roar reached the sky as the leader, who'd circled round with the mother of an ornate ceremonial sword, sliced towards me and connected at the junction of the neck and the wing. Then the fiery tunnel appeared and I dived into it, and back to the Ice Age.

The earth sizzled and the tunnel consumed itself and it faded from the scene, leaving only a distant shriek on the air.

Bert dropped me and fell. Through a miasma of steam his face was green with exhaustion, and a gaping, smouldering mass near his left hip showed an ugly wound where he'd held me and dragged me back. A dryad tended him, stuffing green into the gaping hole. A gentle trickle down my chest showed that I'd brought back the wound I'd sustained whilst in dragon-mode.

I yanked some sphagnum moss from my depleted wren

bag to staunch the wound, and tossed some in Bert's direction. The dryads had withdrawn, obviously scared after my last transmogrification. I followed the gaze of a bold one: through my belt I seemed to have stuck the arm of the last dryad I'd grabbed as I became the dragon. It was a stick of charcoal, still warm.

I looked around the landscape. Whilst I'd been gone, the earth had continued heaving gently, and the last of the dead bikers were disappearing like worms into their holes, along with their bikes and the apparatus of the factory. For the rest, the central fire-inferno had burnt any evidence which hadn't been swept away in the first torrent. The place was cleansing itself: looked like anything else we could do would be supererogatory.

Time for the off. I hunkered down to help Bert.

Suddenly, the sky lit up like neon, and the lines of power that had faithfully maintained since the beginning started flickering like the gas lamp at the edge of Narnia. Bert's Green Ray was the most stable, ironically. Greensleeves and Ruari must have been hit by the backlash from the magical battle, and I didn't stop to imagine what would happen to us Strangers in a Strange Land if the lines disappeared.

I grabbed Bert: it was like trying to shift an old tree trunk, and he groaned like an ancient oak, tortured by a gale. In desperation I pulled again and a lone dryad, with one arm, shimmied forward to add her weight.

Emboldened, the others joined in and I stood, propping Bert who was bent double over his wound.

The dryads surrounded us, their lissome green limbs like a wickerwork support as I placed my hand over his third eye and withdrew my attention from the scene before me.

The bones of the land
The blood of the sea
The breath of the sky...

I felt my blood-beat.
 Bert's image of his homeland rose and helped me to make a firm fix on where we were bound: home, before we lost our chance. His home. The heather, the dim light of the moor at dusk, and, in the middle, a green castle, melding into the landscape. In my mind, I paced the land, its energies rising through my body, and the pull was reinforced by my own images of beech trees, the forest of the south, Hestia, the Disney-Fantasia-verdant paradise which was the world in my own time, far from this cold, pristine beauty.

A fog settled around us and the dryads withdrew slowly: again I was stretched between heaven and earth in a glowing column of light and from the horizons the rays streamed strongly. A curtain of mist thinned and golden light streamed through: the blessed light of the present day. The Earth Dragon heaved beneath our feet, the wings of the Air Dragon pushed at my back, and my longing was so great that I lifted Bert effortlessly through.

16
East, west, bothy's best

An explosion rent the sky as we found ourselves back on the moor. The wet, cold, miserable, glorious, blessed moor, the same as when we'd left it. I opened my parched throat to the healing saturation of the air.

As the thunder rolled away, a fork of lightning heralded another loud clap, and the heavens opened. Within a minute, we were wading in sodden heather, making for the bothy. The lightnings shone like Very lights with the afterglow of my changing from my fiery last incarnation, making a red wash over the moor - The Red Glen. As it faded, we heard over the storm the most welcome sound in the world: the whoops and calls of our two friends. Two mud monsters met in the middle distance and slithered towards us, and they swept along with the wind and rain, into our tight embrace: Ruari, Greensleeves, Gwion and Bert. Our soaking heads made a dripping flower-mandala.

And then Bert sagged.

We staggered under the dead weight, and, under Greensleeves' direction, laid him on his stomach on the sopping heather, wincing at his groans. From Green Knight to Wounded King in one fell swoop, I thought grimly, as the lady tended him, packing out the dryad's compress with more greenery. And what does that mean for the land now? Unnervingly, he pierced me with a look as if he was reading my mind: I quickly imaged a bright mirror over my third eye. We'd been on the same side so far, but a man's got to protect himself.

After three deep breaths, he seemed to revive and curled round into a foetal position, and then levered himself up to sitting.

"Whoa, that's good, girl: you always know what I need," he commended her ministrations, whilst Ruari looked on. This adventure seemed to have distanced him from his infatuation, and his eyes were clear with just a suggestion of the Compassion Ray as he propped Bert against a hairy shin and wet kilt. That was one less loose end for me to tie up, then, I thought, mentally consigning my 'love-lorn/love-gorn' spell back into its box. Just as well: I'd have done my best for my cousin, but that sort of messing often turns out badly.

"Get on with you," she chided affectionately, "I might have trusted you to stick your nose in; when little Gwion only asked you along to make up the numbers.

I refused to look shamefaced. How could I have known what a powerhouse he'd be? I knew what I - and the world - owed to this strange troll-like figure.

"Your staff!" Suddenly Ruari exclaimed. "Where did you leave it?"

Bert gestured to his starting point of the rite, and, without a word, my cousin made his way over the heather. I wearily reached into the wren bag and set a mini bat-detect sonar-search off in his wake: it would soon overtake him and show him the quickest way.

Bert had that Hibernian grin which I distrusted so much. His next words proved what I'd thought; amongst his untapped talents was a certain facility for mind-reading.

"Well, brother, you may be right about my transformation, that remains to be seen: but, knight or wounded king, the best place for me now is Hautdesert: if the missus will help me?"

She smiled assent. If I wondered how the hell an eight stone woman would manhandle a troll for miles over the moor in a storm, I was too polite to ask. I heard ravens gathering, and the heather was looking perceptibly greener. I felt that I'd overdosed on magic for the moment: with my assignment sorted, time for me to retire and leave the locals to it.

As I reached the bothy door, Bert called me back.
"Gwion: you did well for a Sassanach. The Land thanks you." He raised himself enough to give a half bow and to my surprise, madam curtsied. "And I'm sorry I couldn't get you back from that hell's coven as soon as you wanted: what with you yelling like a salamander mating with a grampus down the time/space continuum and all."

I reddened: transmogrifying into a totem animal is private stuff, and take that to the power of a thousand when it's a dragon: and I didn't want to be reminded, in company, of how I'd behaved. But he was carrying on regardless: "Reckon that we're even Stevens, though."

As I looked mystified, he gestured to the scar on his neck. So long ago it seemed now: the beginning of our adventure. A lifetime.
I felt my own neck, where the blood from the magician's sword gash had coagulated: I'd have a fine scar there myself, soon. So had he left me there a second too late on purpose? Was this the Scottish version of blood brothers? I was too tired to ask.

"Go well Green Knight," I bowed, "Lady," and walked through the bothy entrance. Turning to shut the door, I wasn't surprised to see the moor empty, but for a bird wheeling overhead.

The spot between my shoulderblades prickled: time I was out of this ancient place, with its blood bonds and mysteries. Like Hannay in The Thirty nine Steps, I just wanted to be back on my own turf, but we seemed to have lost a day whilst in the past: night was falling and I had some serious rest arrears to make up.

It was the work of a few minutes to make up the fire with peats and stuff rags into the ceiling withies to stop the drips. I stripped off my robe and sank down by the fire. Soon Ruari would be along, and, in that mysterious way that these people had, would magic food and rest from this unprepossessing shack. The fire flared, and I swung the kettle across. Under the workbench with his paraphernalia I saw blankets and some pallets.

As I made space for the makeshift bed, a hum rose in my throat, of overwhelming gratitude: the first that I'd used on these moors, which had guided me safely to my cousin's door. I thought of the fae moths and the warmth of my welcome; of the tenacity of the dryads and the little sulky heather, who'd entwined the black knight's ankles and rendered them helpless at a crucial time. Of such small things are battles won.

And then it was just me and the firelight in the coals of the peat, with molten towers rising and ashes wheeling like hawks over the moors in the depths of the fire: relationship, exchange, and a deep peace that told me that I'd finished the job, and done well.

Next morning, Ruari told me that I was out for the count by the time he got back. He'd tried to push me over to make room for himself on the bed, but backed off sharpish when I turned, deep in sleep, with my arms outstretched and the smile of a lover on my face.

Through my dreams, a green lady, her sturdy boots replaced by silken slippers, danced sensuously with Dryads and we drank deeply of the wine of the sap, whilst a mysterious piping figure watched from afar, smiling.

The Lord of the Land toasted me from the couch where he rested, the bloom of healing already in his face; the lady swung me into the dance and wrapped her green girdle around me.

And although I could see from the moor and the heather that I was in foreign Scotland, I knew deep within my being that I had gained another home.

AFTERWORD

It was in the magical landscape of Priddy in Somerset that I first met Gwion Dubh, and over a few days whilst he helped out at the Sheep Fair we talked long into the night. These two stories are the first result of those meetings.

Those evenings are potent memories: a bright fire and darkness beyond, with no traffic from the Old Bristol Road to disturb the clink of mugs, the soft cadences of Gwion's voice and the occasional screech of an owl - always at the most apposite points in his story. Those who practice Druid ritual will recognise this phenomenon. The gypsy encampment that was his temporary home was the kingdom of his old mate, a horse- and road-man who's been travelling this island since the 1970s.... Thanks for the hospitality, Pete.   *PB Nov 2007*

The college in Anglesey where Gwion underwent his stringent training is unfortunately not open to the public. For those who would like to learn more about the nuts and bolts of modern Druidry, there is an excellent postal course offered by The Order of Bards, Ovates and Druids, which comes with his highest recommendation: Postal enquiries to the Secretary PO Box 1333 Lewes, E Sussex BN7 1DX
Email: **office@druidry.org**
Website: **www.druidry.org**

For more news of Gwion and all things Druidic, contact the author via the website: www.pennybillington.co.uk